WHOM EVIL TOUCHES

by
D. E. Royce

Whom Evil Touches
This is a work of fiction. All of the characters, events or organizations por-
trayed in this novel are either products of the author's imagination or are used
fictitiously.

ISBN-10: 1484814037
ISBN-13: 9781484814031
Library of Congress Control Number: 2014900142
CreateSpace Independent Publishing Platform
North Charleston, South Carolina

First Edition:
Publisher: Paula L. Darois
Printed in the United States of America
For more information contact: www.deroyce.com

This book is dedicated to my grandmother, Elizabeth, with love and gratitude.

"Fate leads the willing and drags along the reluctant."
—Seneca

PROLOGUE

S tellwagen Bank embodies much of New England's mari-
time history. Tens of thousands of years before the U.S.
Navy loaned Lieutenant Commander Henry Stellwagen
to the U.S. Coast Survey to map the waters off the New
England coast, the great Laurentide Glacier stretched its
vast ice sheet southeast from the barren and bitter tundra
of Canada, northern United States and Greenland, scouring
what is now New Brunswick and Massachusetts.

An incredible two miles high, the ice sheet reached across
New England and crept to a frosty halt over Cape Cod, that
long, sweeping, sickle-shaped landmass that defines the
southernmost point of Massachusetts Bay. Stellwagen Bank
lay due north and east of the Cape.

Once home to windswept grasses, towering pines, and
prehistoric mammals, it, too, froze in time - a long time,
nearly fifteen thousand years. Then, true to the innate quali-
ties of opposites, Laurentide's ominous ice sheet gave way to
the warmth of the sun and earth and retreated; sweating at
first, the ice melted.

Eerie groans and ear-splitting sounds from shifting ice
packs echoed for hundreds of miles. Slowly, its huge, glistening, white body gushed immense volumes of moisture. It

returned to the soil and oceans the enormous boulders, silt, and seeds that had lain in its path and been dragged thousands of miles across the continents, then stilled beneath its frozen domain for tens of thousands of years.

The great thaw gave life to a new land: green mountains and lush valleys, granite hills, and fragrant meadows of soft grasses and wild flowers. Crystal-clear ponds and lakes evolved from the great depressions in the earth that had borne the weight of Laurentide's icy body. The overflow saturated the silt below and gave rise to swift, mighty rivers that now flow south and southeast and filter through the saltwater marshes that inhabit the rocky coastline and peaceful bays of New England before washing into the Atlantic Ocean with the flow of the day's tides. It has been estimated that when the land decompressed, Laurentide raised the Atlantic's sea level by over 350 feet.

Lands that once rose above the ocean lay beneath it, and the great expanse of ocean that lies between the New England coastline and Northern Europe—3,000 miles of it—became one of the world's richest fishing grounds and greatest trade routes between the continents. Stellwagen Bank, an underwater plateau, sprawls 26 miles north to south, between Cape Ann and Cape Cod, its southern width measures 13 miles and its northern portion, about 3 miles. Water depths, at the top of the bank, measure 60 - 125 feet below the surface, and closer to the ports of Boston, around 300 feet. Further northeast, near dead center of the bank, dark, muddy canyons exceed 600 feet in depth.

The bank, plateau, and underwater current create a splendid sequence of events that supply the area with abundant marine life. The steeper sides of the plateau cause deep-water currents to rise when it hits the bank, sending surges of nutrients and minerals from the ocean's bottom that feed the ecosystem.

Seventeenth-century New England settlers harvested Stellwagen's bounty of fin and shellfish, cod, flounder, and haddock. Whaling ships from Gloucester, New Bedford, Plymouth, Provincetown and Salem hunted whales and tuna.

Swift schooners loaded with granite from the quarries of Quincy and Rockport, Massachusetts navigated through Stellwagen to carry their precious cargos to Europe and Asia and returned to Boston with coal, silk, mahogany, and china. Supplies for shelter and adornments for the home and body were not the only supplies unloaded in New England ports.

Boston's strategic location was not lost on the rum-runners and bootleggers during Prohibition, when Americans were lawfully denied alcohol. FBI agents accompanied by tongue-in-cheek police officers stormed illegal distilleries, shattering with sledgehammers and axes vats of aging whiskey, bourbon, and beer. This enforcement gave life to a new breed of entrepreneurs: the rum-runner.

Unlike their bootlegger counterparts who utilized the land for transporting their contraband stuffed in leather boots or positioned with care in the garters, bras, and girdles of voluptuous females who carried it by train, truck, car, and wagon, rum-runners took to the sea. Resourceful and well organized, they countered the attack on their liberties and converted excursion, fishing, and ragtag pleasure boats into receiver ships for the lucrative business of supplying liquor-deprived Americans with scotch, whiskey, bourbon, and champagne.

The plan was simple: supplier boats from Europe whisked the spirits across the Atlantic and unloaded them onto waiting receiver ships anchored in the shallow waters of Stellwagen, which then transported it to Boston for distribution.

And there were plenty of risk takers - rum-running was a lucrative business. An honest, hardworking guy in the 1920s made an average of $50 a week. Running intoxicants brought in the decent sum of $300 a week. A rum-running captain could easily bank $200,000 a year, compared to the dedicated captains of the U.S. Coast Guard, who earned about $6,000.

On any given run, suppliers in Europe shipped an estimated $250,000 worth of alcohol across the Atlantic, bound for the East Coast. One of the grand schemers who assured that it reached its destination was William S. McCoy, who controlled nearly all distribution. He bought at auction a schooner, named *Arethusa,* in Gloucester, Massachusetts, renamed it *Tomaka*, installed a larger engine, mounted a machine gun on deck, and refitted the stinking fish pens below deck to ship his cargo securely.

He employed larger and faster receiver ships. Unlike his counterparts, who were prone to diluting the booze with water for extra profits, the non-drinking McCoy delivered the spirits in full proof. He was a man who kept his word and provided the real deal. No wonder many historians credit the adage, "the real McCoy," with his name.

On November 15, 1923, McCoy opened fire on a coast guard crew attempting to board his ship. The coast guard returned fire and the *Tomaka* took a fatal hit in the hull. McCoy took a hit in his earnings. His days of rum-running ended. The coast guard won the battle, and, eventually, the war.

A year or so later, on a crisp, clear evening in October, while lying in wait off the coast of Boston Harbor, the coast guard spotted a flotilla of twelve receiver ships anchored in the shallow waters of Stellwagen. Alert, on guard, and armed, the rum-runners eyed their enemy. It has been said that from the Bunker Hill Monument in Charlestown or atop the hill on Thomas Park in South Boston, one could see the red-hot muzzle glow from the machine guns' fire when all hell broke loose.

The rum-runners dumped 850 tons of their liquid gold into the dark waters and took up defensive positions. Determined and steadfast, the coast guard braved the knife-wielding, gun-toting rum-runners, boarded their craft, and hauled them to Boston for arraignment.

The history of Stellwagen is rich with similar personal accounts and seaworthy yarns. Most were fortunate; others, not so lucky. The crew of the 742-ton, USCGD *Paulding*, patrolling the waters off Cape Cod for rum-runners, proved less successful, and in a tragic accident, rammed and sank a US Navy submarine.

One need only journey below the watery surface of this bountiful seascape to the bottom, where the flounder and lobster feed and the drone of powerboats and diesel-driven trawlers are barely heard, to view a repository of marine history. Shipwrecks and china, cannon balls and pistols, harpoons and machine guns, wedding bands and bottles of champagne: relics of bold beginnings and ill-fated endings, all gone down to the sea in disaster.

Not all artifacts rest gently or remain forever in watery graves below Stellwagen. Some degrade into the salty brine or provide life-giving nutrients to aquatic creatures. Others travel by the gentle persuasion of local currents. Some may eventually reach the Gulf Stream's current, which begins its journey in Mexico, rounds the southern tip of Florida, and flows up along the East Coast, then drifts northeast and diagonally across Stellwagen and three thousand miles across the open Atlantic to the shores of England.

It was thought that Judy Lydon Kennedy's body made such a trip, although not as long because it did not start in Mexico. Hers began in Quincy, Massachusetts - in Quincy Bay. A few parts of her body never made it across the pond, so to speak. They did, however, make it into what one would call unsuitable locations, meaning unfit for any human being, living or dead.

CHAPTER ONE

D etective Sweede Swenson and his fellow investigators
spent nearly every Saturday during July, August and
September on his Bayliner, fishing out at Stellwagen—today
was no different.

Ronan sat bundled in a bright orange life jacket on the
rear deck. Exhausted and heavy with sleep, he closed his
weary eyes and turned his elegant black face to the wind and
the cooling sprays of salt water that soothed it. He moved
his head a bit from the heat of the sun's rays and fell asleep
to the monotonous drone of the boat's engines.

Sweede turned from his high seat at the steering wheel
and looked back. "Boy, Ronan's wiped out."

Gillan Murphy gulped his beer and nodded. "We've been
working steady for three days and pulled 820 pounds of dope
and a damn arsenal of assault weapons off an oil tanker yesterday morning. We spent the day before that at Our Lady of
the Atlantic, securing it for the bishop's big speech."

"Find anything?"

Gillan burst into a hearty laugh. "Yeah, empty nip bottles
of vodka in all the confessionals!"

"Too bad today wasn't as easy," said Sweede, guiding his
craft away from the sailboats ahead.

Gillan shook his head. "It's never easy before vacation. It was a real mess up there today. Four dead bodies, a booby-trapped bomb, and the hull of my police boat shot up. We've never had any trouble with the families that vacation on that island. All you need is a couple of bad actors staying up there to mess up a good thing."

He turned back and contemplated Ronan still sleeping among the noisy chatter and laughter of Sweede's fishing buddies. "That dog saved my life and the life of every other cop there. Those little creeps put a booby-trapped bomb right inside the door to the cottage. If one of us had opened it...*bah boom!*"

Sweede let out a long, low, whistle. "That dog's unbelievable; all that training sure pays off. And you still drill him every day, Gil?"

"Yup, every damn day. Hey, Sweede, didn't you arrest a dealer coming off that island a few years ago, a Shawn something? He was carrying a Glock."

"Oh yeah, his name is Shawn Yee. He's out on parole. He has really nice parents, too. They don't know what the hell to do with him. He's always in trouble."

"Not anymore. He was one of the punks taken out today. Ronan tracked him down."

Gillan rubbed his head and yawned. "What a day! Glad you were in the area to pick me up. I knew you guys were out fishing at Stellwagen, and I didn't feel like hooking a ride with the coast guard. Where are you headed to now?"

Sweede glanced at the clock. "We're headed for the yacht club, going to catch the game. Want us to drop you off at Squantum or Marina Bay?"

"No. I'll go to Hough's Neck with you guys. Marybeth can pick me up down there; she's still packing for our trip to Bar Harbor."

Gillan yawned again, gave a good long reach, and picked up his beer. "Sweede, I've got to stretch my legs. I'll go say hi to the guys." He made his way to the rear deck and plopped himself beside Ronan. He was asleep in five minutes.

Sweede eased the throttle forward, and the gleaming white Bayliner took off, skimming like a silk ribbon over the ocean. Its sleek bow cut into the glistening red reflections of the late day's sun and spangled across the rolling swells, softly showering the sun-parched fishing party. Hearty sounds of laughter rose behind him.

He smiled and took a swig of ice-cold beer. God, he felt good. It was a perfect day - all blue skies and sunshine and no wind; a perfect fishing day but not for the purists and their sailboats.

Ted Smith clenched a cigar between his teeth, staggered to Sweede, and smacked him on the back. "Hey, how many years have we been fishing at Stellwagen?"

Sweede furrowed his brow. "Since we were seven or eight. I remember going out there on Sunday mornings with your father. We didn't have to go that far before then. The bay wasn't polluted, and we could still hook a haddock in our backyard, for crying out loud."

Ted puffed on his cigar and swayed forward. "I wouldn't have wanted to grow up anywhere else."

Sweede nodded. "Me either. When you think of it, Ted, every kid in the neighborhood learned to swim, sail, screw, and drink behind the seawall at the end of my street. I'm glad

I still live there. I wake up and the first thing I see is the bay. It's probably why I joined the navy."

Three tours of active duty took Sweede far from Quincy Bay—around and below the world's waterways - to exotic lands and ports classified by naval intelligence as "none of anyone's business." His last tour ended aboard a diesel-driven submarine in a fleet, called the Grey Ghosts, and he aptly named his Bayliner just that: *The Grey Ghost*.

The day's sun dropped lower in the western sky, and Sweede inched the throttle forward again. *The Grey Ghost* accelerated with the grace and precision of his Ferrari, powered by the soft roar of the twin Mercs. He took another gulp of beer and rested the ice-cold bottle in its holder. "Do you have any more cigars?"

Ted sliced the tip off a Churchill and handed it to Sweede. "Here you go."

He took a few puffs and sat back. "It doesn't get any better than this Ted."

"No, it doesn't. Look at those seagulls."

Their feathers were tinged a bright pink from the late afternoon's sunlight, as they circled high above the boat, showing off their soft white underbellies. They soared ever higher, hitched a draft, and leisurely drifted over the sea.

Sweede watched them move in slow, mesmerizing circles - around and around - high above the rolling blue swells below them. He yawned and leaned back in his seat, gazing at their airy show.

Ronan awoke, rose abruptly, and anxiously sniffed the air.

Sweede's body stiffened; there it was again: a subtle drag in the boat's movement and a quick hitch in velocity. The engines screeched, sputtered, and shimmied, gave one horrendous jerk and heaved *The Grey Ghost* to a dead halt. Thick, fat clouds of black smoke poured from aft into the oncoming wind, and then gusted into the faces of the horrified band of boaters.

They grabbed their beers and scrambled for cover. When the smoke cleared and its last streams wafted over their heads, Sweede called for a sea tow and waited. The soothing sound of the waves gently lapping against *The Grey Ghost* did not calm Sweede.

To the west, the last of the day's blazing sun slipped below the skyline and a chilly northeast wind gusted. Sweede stood in the dusk, hands resting on his hips, legs spread like eagles' wings, unconsciously shifting the weight of his strapping frame to the rhythmic rocking of *The Grey Ghost*. His ice-blue eyes narrowed at the sight of the soot-blackened deck.

The silence was earsplitting.

•••

Some twenty five miles south of Sweede and his *Grey Ghost*, near the Scituate side of Marshfield, the evening's dusk rolled in with the tide. Manny Aruda and his young daughter waited for the police; they'd made a discovery—a gruesome discovery. A patrol car screeched to a halt near the pier.

Manny hastily grabbed his daughter's hand and breathlessly stumbled to his boat. "Don't step on that, officer! My daughter threw up there, she's so upset. My wife's coming to get her. Stand over here Olivia—beside me—don't look, don't look." He nervously patted her back. "Here, hide your face in my jacket Olivia. Close your eyes and hide your face!" Manny wiped the tears from his eyes and blew his nose. "Officer, we were out about a half mile checking my lobster traps and found something on one of them." He pointed to the trap on the deck of his boat. The young officer clicked on his flashlight and slowly stepped forward. Manny anxiously blessed himself. "It's up on the left side, sir, near the top, stuck in the net. Oh, God have mercy!"

The officer cautiously crouched down and aimed the glaring light closer to the top of the trap. "Holy smoke, you're right—it's a hand, it's a woman's hand!"

CHAPTER TWO

Will Kennedy slid his bright red kayak from the racks atop the roof of his black Jeep, positioned it with care in the garage and stuffed his wetsuit and nose clips in the trash. In the morning, he would stop at Geary's for a new wet suit. The water was cold for this time of year.

At fifty-six, Kennedy was trim, strong as an ox, and graceful as a gazelle. He understood the mechanics of a body in motion and moved with purpose and grace. Will wasn't a bad cook either and began beating eggs for an omelet. He wanted to eat and leave the kitchen before his wife, Judy came home. He heard the slam of the screen door and a sweet, small voice calling to him.

"Hi, Mr. Kennedy. Do you have any Band-Aids?"

Will turned, smiling. "Hi, Suzanne, what are you up to?"

She brushed the tumbling curls from her face and mournfully lifted her leg. "This is what I'm up to. Look at my knee!"

"Did you fall off your bike?"

Suzanne sniffled and wiped her eyes. "Yes, Mr. Kennedy, I did. I hit a bump! And my hands are scratched too. See!" She spread her reddened palms before his eyes and then wiped the tears from her own. "We don't have any Band-Aids. The babysitter called my mother. She'll bring some home, but I can't wait." She plunked herself down on the floor and sat brooding over the abrasion on her knee.

Will hid his smile and tenderly examined her knee and hands. "I'll have you fixed up in no time."

"Where's your dog; where's Bosco?"

Will looked away from her. "Suzanne, Bosco was sick. I had to put him to sleep."

"He was pretty old, Mr. Kennedy. He had white whiskers on his nose. We had to put our dog to sleep too. My mother and father said that they go to dog heaven, and it's a good place for them. They run around and play Frisbee all day and can chew on as many bones as they want!"

Will nodded. "Suzanne, your parents are right. How's your brother's bike running?"

"Oh, good since you fixed the wheel. My dad will be over to pay you for it when he gets home."

"Tell your dad I'm all set."

"I will, but he'll come over anyway. Where's Mrs. Kennedy?"

"She had to go away on business in Georgia, and then she went to Florida."

"Is she going to Disney World?"

"I'm not sure, but, I don't think so. She'll let you know when she comes home. She should be here pretty soon."

"You can let me know, Mr. Kennedy. I like you. My mother says you're a good man, just like my dad. And besides, I don't think Mrs. Kennedy likes anybody very much, especially little kids like me!"

"Do you want some peppermint patties to take home?"

She dug into the candy and fumbled to fill her pockets.

"Here, let me put those in a little bag. You can carry it home in the basket on your bike."

"That's a good idea, Mr. Kennedy!" She grabbed the bag but quickly placed it on the table. "I have to check one thing before I go." Suzanne peeked under the Band-Aid. "My knee stopped bleeding!" She beamed up at Will, took his hand, and walked him outside to her bike. He gently placed the candy in the basket and watched her peddle home to wait for her mother and father.

He glanced at the clock; Judy should be home any minute. Will carried his omelet and newspaper to his study and closed the door. His last conversation with Judy had instantly turned ugly, and he had not heard from her since - a week - and what a relief!

It had been this way for years now, maybe nine or ten. Yes, ten; ten years of constant quarreling, being baited into arguments, false accusations, chronic aggravation, and distance, a chilly, emotional detachment that left him confused, insecure, and not knowing how to act around her.

Will knew that she still blamed him for Jamie's death, even though the doctor had assured her that no one was at fault. She had miscarried four times since Jamie, until Dr. Wingard finally said, "No more."

Judy spent the next couple of years lying on the couch crying, sleeping, or screaming at Will. He had coaxed her into counseling, and she went year after year to no avail and refused to take medication.

They turned to adoption agencies but were deemed unsuitable after thorough background checks. Will cautiously approached the subject of the child Judy had given up for adoption years earlier. Maybe the connection would help, but it was a mistake. She flew into a rage that lasted for weeks and turned on him forever.

Now, he felt calmed by her absence but on guard in her presence. The brittle civility that existed between them was suffocating, but Will Kennedy found ways to deal with it, mainly by flying under her high-pitched radar.

Judy knew what he was doing but mistook his passiveness for weakness. She thought a pro wrestler would envy her chokehold on Will but was wrong.

He simply didn't care anymore or feel the need to justify his behavior or challenge her twisted opinions and logic. Will thought about leaving Judy a million times but had too much money at stake, too little confidence, and enough guilt about her state of mind and its causes to stay put.

Nor did he fool around. Will ignored the teasing touches and come-on glances from the girls he knew at the running club and endless fundraisers and chamber breakfasts he attended. In his heart, Will longed for a love he could count on, a love he could wrap his arms around in the middle of the night, a love with whom he could feel safe.

His study, business, running, and swimming offered safe havens from Judy. Will had bought a cleaning business some twenty years ago and now made decent money. His crew of techs, mostly Russians, cleaned offices on the South Shore and parts of South Boston and Dorchester where he had grown up.

They had introduced him to the art of playing chess and met every Tuesday night in the quiet comfort of Will's spacious study, which occupied most of the second floor of the oversized cape. It was peaceful there, day or night, season after season, chess or no chess.

He savored the hilltop location, the sense of being closer to the open sky and a balcony view of gray squirrels engaged in daring, acrobatic leaps from tree to tree and wire to wire. His chessboard lay on a table to the right of a picture window that showcased the tall columns of bristling pine trees that dotted the backyard.

Soft, leather, cream-colored, easy chairs stood before the fieldstone fireplace, lined on both sides with shelves of books and keepsakes. When November's chill filled the air, Will built a fire and basked in the hypnotic high that the flickering flames induced in him. In the sweltering heat of summer evenings, he relaxed there alone in the darkness, content in the southeast breeze that billowed the curtains and flowed over his body.

The gentle wind soothed his thoughts while the summer's night voices of the chirping crickets, croaking bull frogs, and come-here mating song of the mockingbird stirred his soul. Will Kennedy felt his God in their presence.

He gathered his newspaper and dinner plate and headed downstairs to the kitchen. It was nearly ten, and the door to Judy's bedroom was still open. She hadn't returned. Will read for a while, marked the page, let out a good yawn, and shut off the light.

Streams of words and conversations of yesterday and today jumbled together. New faces and distant faces, memories of people and places far away returned to his dreams in shades of soft gray and lavender. He and Christine walked in the snow and rain, laughing, gentle fingers caressing tender eyelids, touching soft, moist lips, regrets, fleeting years, too few left.

When his breaths came slowly and gently, and the muscles beneath his skin melded into the softness around him, the minstrels of the night cast their spell of sweet relief from his mind's wandering, and he slept peacefully. It's been said that a clear conscience makes the softest pillow, and Will's handsome head lay on such a pillow.

At 5:00 A.M., he awoke with a jolt, hustled to the kitchen, started the coffee and glanced into Judy's room. Her bed was still made. After finishing his breakfast, he called her, left a message, and went to work. Will checked his messages a couple of times during the day, but there was no reply from Judy.

He eventually telephoned Alfred Locke, President of Quincy Quarry Bank and Trust, where Judy worked. He and Alfred got along pretty well. Occasionally, they played racquetball, a few rounds of golf, or swam laps at the Atlantic Club in the winter.

"No, Will, uh, I don't believe she was on bank business, uh, unless something came up that I was unaware of and Crombie sent her to Atlanta, though I have no idea why he would have done such a thing. Our clerks are trained right here in the conference room, and their yearly in-services are provided here as well.

"I may have misunderstood, but I thought she asked for time off to travel with you to a chess match in Quebec. I was away the week prior to her vacation, so we didn't speak before she left. Crombie is out today, having a colonoscopy. I'll call him later and get back to you."

Locke called Will around 6:00 P.M. "Will, Alfred Locke here. I spoke with Crombie; Judy wasn't sent anywhere on banking business. Crombie thought she was vacationing in Arizona."

"Thanks, Al, I'll figure it out." He swallowed hard and felt a searing heat move over his neck and face. A ferocious hammering of his heart banged in his ears. Will fumbled with his phone, put it down, sat down, picked it up again, and pressed the keys.

"I need to report my wife as missing."

CHAPTER THREE

Christine O'Malley huddled over the foot rests of the wheel chair and fiddled with its levers. Instead of pulling them up and out, she pushed them down and pressed in, the extra wide wheel chair collapsed. She hauled it into the trunk of her car, slammed the cover, hastily brushed her hands together, took a deep breath, and cautiously slid into the front seat.

"Well Mom, what did you think?"

Rose glanced down, drew from her purse a meticulously pressed and scented handkerchief, and handed it to Christine. "I think you should wash your hands and then take your dress to the cleansers. You should have been more careful lifting my wheelchair."

"You didn't like it?"

Rose clutched her purse and gazed ahead.

"Mom, you didn't like it?"

"Christine, it looks like rain. I don't think you drive so well in the rain, neither could your father. Let Natalie drive, or better still, call Phillip."

Natalie looked out the window and then flipped a page of her magazine. "Ma, they're fair weather clouds, and, besides, I like sitting in the back seat. I hate driving, and there's nothing wrong with Christine's driving. And there was nothing wrong with Daddy's driving. Phillip is busy. You never got your license, what do you know about driving?"

Rose's face hardened. She clenched her teeth and crossed her arms over her enormous breasts. "I want to go home. I need to take my blood pressure pill at exactly two o'clock."

Natalie checked her Rolex and leaned over the front seat. "Step on it Christine! Ma's house is almost a mile away, and we've only got forty- five minutes to get there!"

Christine chuckled.

Rose glared at her then struggled to turn to Natalie. "Oh go ahead, gang up on me! You two are nothing but a couple big shots; a lawyer and a psychologist— a family counselor no less, trying to get rid of me—trying to stick me into some nursing home!"

She closed her eyes and gripped the gleaming gold crucifix that hung from her neck and dipped into her cleavage. "Mark my words: both of you will have blood on your hands!"

Natalie opened a compact and touched up her lipstick. "Guilt doesn't work anymore, Ma," she said blandly and snapped shut the mirror. "We've been talking about this for three years: you won't live with either of us, you won't accept help in the house, and all you eat are candy bars and cookies.

"The fire department has picked you up off the floor five times since Easter, and now you've fractured your hip. You're running out of options! And Marsh House at Hingham Harbor is not a nursing home. It's an assisted living. It's brand new. The food is great and you'll be with friends.

"The activities director will take you shopping and on day trips. You can play bridge, take art lessons, enjoy cocktail hour, and have your own garden, if you want. People are willing to entertain you and help you in any way they can. You need to be safe. You need to make a decision!"

Rose clutched her handbag. "I'm sure they'll do everything for me—for a price! Who wouldn't? Do you think I'm stupid?"

"Money isn't the issue, and you know it," snapped Natalie.

Christine sighed. "Mom, Aunt Amelia lives there, Mrs. Cappola and Mrs. Saluti both live there, and Mr. Indelicato just moved in. They all love it, and they can't wait for you to move in. Everyone is so pleasant.

"It's the third time we've toured there. Our lunch was delicious, the staff seems professional, and the nurses wear those long white jackets over their clothes."

She drew a quick breath and continued. "The apartment they showed us is lovely. It overlooks the harbor. We can call the decorator before we move your furniture in. It will be fun!"

Rose wrinkled her nose. "Aunt Amelia has always been jealous of me, and the other two are low class. Jean Coppola is a pig that wears too much perfume and cheap jewelry, and she chews with her mouth open. Sally Saluti swears like a man and uses the F-word all the time. I heard her use it at her own husband's wake! I don't know what Tony ever saw in her. She's vulgar and disrespectful!

"And in case you didn't notice, Joe Indelicato's fly was down. I bet he reads those sex magazines; men like him make me sick to my stomach! Your father never did anything like that!"

Natalie ran a file lightly over her nails and smirked at the back of her mother's head. "Yes he did, and he hid them in the cellar!"

"How dare you say such a thing! Your father never!"

"Stop it, just stop it!" cried Christine. She swerved into the driveway, jerked the car into park, cast a wary glance at her mother, and then turned to Natalie.

She slipped the nail file back into its sheath, raised her impeccably shaped eyebrows, and smiled smugly at her sister.

Rose frantically fanned herself with the brochure from Marsh House. "I need to take my pill. I want to take a good nap, if it's A-OK with you two! Just get me into the house!"

Once inside, Christine closed the drapes, and turned a soft, white, blanket up and over her mother's legs and lap. Rose threw it off.

Christine sighed and ran a hand through her hair. "All right, Mom, Natalie and I will start dinner. Phillip and the children will be here at five. I'll wake you up at four."

"Make it four-fifteen," Rose sneered. "And thank God that Phillip is coming. There's no one like your brother!"

Christine wearily headed to the kitchen.

Natalie's voice rang out from the veranda. "I'm out here; let's take a break before starting the roast and salad. I started the sauce. Phil called; he's bringing the raviolis and cheese-cake. Here, I poured a glass of sherry for you."

Christine took a sip, "Is Patty coming with Phillip and the children?"

Natalie shook her head. "No, Patty has had it with Ma's insults, and Phillip supports her decision. He's going to speak to her about it; Ma needs to stop her unwarranted attacks on Patty."

"Yes, she does. There's no need of it."

She kicked off her heels and sank into the well-cushioned lounge chair, thoughtfully looking at the pool's shimmering blue water. "I should have brought my bathing suit."

Natalie yawned lazily. "I was thinking the same thing. A swim would feel good." She settled into her chair while admiring the pear trees on the far side of the yard, the birds and squirrels swooshing and swirling in the leaves. The fruit was nearly ripe and ready for picking, and the wisteria hung heavy and fragrant over the veranda's trellis. Clusters of pink, candy-colored roses fell softly over the rear fence and into Mr. Napoli's back yard.

Christine breathed deeply and inhaled their sweet fragrance. "I think I'll pick a bouquet of roses. They'll make a lovely centerpiece for the dinner table. Mom always had flowers in the house. The pink roses are her favorite. I remember when Daddy planted them. It's still so strange to see his vegetable garden overgrown with weeds. Mom won't let the landscapers touch it."

Natalie clasped her hands over her mouth and yawned again. "Ma still rules. What little she has left to rule over, her kingdom is nearly gone."

Christine lifted her face to the gentle breeze that moved around her and tenderly rustled from their afternoon droop the heat-laden leaves and flowers. "Mom isn't an easy person to live with."

A scornful smile spread across Natalie's face. "She is, if you're her only son and your name is Phillip. Do you remember that kid from South Boston you dated, Will? Will Kennedy? Ma was so insulted when she found out he had a brother named Phillip, who rode horses at some race track in New Jersey that she made Dad use his contacts to check out him and his family!"

It had been years, but Christine felt the same twinge of regret that gripped her any time she thought about Will. "I'll say they checked him out; it was the beginning of the end of my relationship with him.

"They endured his sporadic phone calls and my never-ending tears because of it. They tolerated him not taking me to my high school prom and not having a job, but when he wound up in jail. That was that.

"It was a terrible time in my life, but he was so messed up. He was just a kid. It still hurts that Mom and Dad sent me to Chicago to stay with Aunt Nellie and Uncle Frank just to keep me away from him under the pretense of wanting me to go to Northwestern instead of Emerson. And they wouldn't pay for it unless I went along with it. I know they were just trying to protect me from him."

Natalie straightened in her chair and faced her sister. "That's true Christine, but it turned out all right. I mean, you got your education and had the twins. They're healthy, and you and Jeffrey had a good marriage. He was really supportive and pushed you to go on and get your law degree."

Christine shook her head. "Natalie, I never cared whether or not I had a law degree. I wanted to be a writer, a travel writer. I wanted to live in London, that's what I wanted.

"Jeffrey thought it was a joke. I got my law degree for his sake, and that's what turned into a joke. He was the top dog attorney, and I was nothing but his scribe, writing his opening and closing statements and doing his research, that is, when I wasn't car-pooling, chaperoning field trips or trying to run the house.

"But I learned from it. I'm lucky that Charlie Sudanski hired me. I mean, Jeffrey's death was so sudden and I never dreamed that he gambled as much as he did or that I'd be working to pay college tuitions and a mortgage. He even spent our retirement funds and borrowed on his life insurance to pay off his gambling debts. He never cared about anyone but himself. Jeffrey was a good attorney but a better actor.

"He left me and the twins broke!"

For a long time, Natalie gazed at her sister and hesitated before she spoke. "Christine, I never realized how, ah, unfulfilled—if that's the right word—you felt. I saw the look that crossed your face when I mentioned Will Kennedy. Christine, you're not alone; most women feel the same way about the first love of their life."

Christine shook her head. "Natalie, please don't categorize my feelings. Feelings are relative. You know that. It was different for me and different for you. You loved Brad and then married Bill.

"Brad married Jane and now, you all car-pool your kids to school, go sailing together, and belong to the same clubs. I never had the peace of mind in knowing what happened to Will, whether or not he made it, or that he straightened out, or that he's happy."

CHAPTER FOUR

Sweede Swenson and Ted Smith were sitting hunched over their desks under the yellow glare of fluorescent lights, finishing paperwork on a hit and run when Will's call came in. Sweede rolled his eyes, pointed to his wristwatch, and then cupped his hand over the mouthpiece.

"Want to bring the car around? We should be at Fenway by six; this call is going to be quick."

Ted nodded and sprinted to the garage.

"This is Detective Swenson."

"Yes, ah, I, I, need to report my wife as missing."

"Who am I speaking to?"

"This is Will Kennedy, and my wife's name is Judy Kennedy."

"How long has she been gone?"

"She left home a week ago and was due back yesterday afternoon. She's about five feet and three inches, 150 pounds, has reddish-colored hair, and wears glasses. She's wearing a gold wedding band and..."

"Hold on there, Mr. Kennedy. You said she left home. Where was she going?"

"She said she was going to Atlanta on business but didn't go."

Sweede's curiosity piqued.

"What do you mean, she didn't go?"

"She told me she was going to Atlanta on banking business and then to Florida for a few days with friends. I spoke with her boss. There was no banking business in Atlanta. They never sent her there."

"Well, have you called her friends?"

Sweede sensed a hesitation in Will's reply. He checked himself, hoping that Will had not heard the trace of amusement in his voice.

"No, she didn't say what friends she was meeting with."

"Have you called her family?"

"She's an only child. Her parents are dead, and she has no aunts or uncles."

"Any cousins?"

"No aunts or uncles usually means no cousins."

Sweede ignored the snipe and checked his watch. "Mr. Kennedy, I've got enough preliminary information to make inquiries. I'll get back to you tomorrow. If your wife shows up before then, give me a call. If not, come on in and fill out the paperwork." He scribbled Will's number on his note pad, grabbed his jacket, and bolted to his waiting car.

Ted and Sweede met the other officers and detectives near the statue of the Splendid Splinter, Teddy 'Ball Game' Williams, who would always rule over Fenway Park.

"The night's on us, Ted. Happy fiftieth."

He shook their hands warmly. "I hope Rivera gets a few innings in for the Yankees. He's a perfect machine: no steroids, no controversy, and humble too."

Sweede broke in. "Yeah, what a break from the usual big mouths most athletes become after a few good seasons.

Their salaries get bigger, and then they stink and still want more money. The owners should sit them down with their agents and play back their crappy games and then negotiate."

"I think that's what they do, Sweede."

"Well, it doesn't work. I like football better anyway," he grumbled.

Sweede leaned into his seat and scanned the night sky. A silver sliver of a new moon hung over third base. He surveyed the beauty of the ballpark and the Sox logo manicured into the field. Food hawkers called out and hustled up and down the narrow stairs, delivering popcorn, hotdogs, and cold drinks to eager Sox fans.

What a night! It was seventy-four degrees and dry with no threat of rain tonight or for the next few days. Sweede passed a hot dog to Ted.

"Sure you don't want to go fishing on Saturday? The flounders are making a comeback."

"No, think I'll pass. I've got to get that garage finished. I can't cook up another excuse for not working on it again this week-end."

"For Christ's sake, Ted, you're going to have plenty of time after next week. You're on vacation for two weeks. If she's pissed, she'll get over it. You've been working on that garage for six years, another day isn't going to matter!"

Ted swigged his beer and laughed. "That's right. Count me in!"

Sweede had never been married and didn't want to be, especially if he wound up like most of his buddies who were trapped in a bad marriage, then divorced, and left broke. He had been in love once, maybe twice, but could not take the next step. The mere thought suffocated him.

Friday came, and Sweede checked around but found nothing relating to the missing Judy Kennedy. He called Will and told him so. "Look, if you don't hear from her by tomorrow morning, call me. If I come up with anything, I'll be in touch."

True to his word, Sweede did keep in touch, and the reason he did, gave him the creeps. He was not a guy who got the creeps or believed in coincidence. Even so, creepy coincidence does happen, as Sweede would soon discover.

CHAPTER FIVE

Will Kennedy had not always been at peace with himself, the law, or cops who enforced its boundaries on his long-past adolescent behavior. Once Will grew up and finally ceased-fire on himself and a society he once so bitterly loathed, he realized that he had learned from it in more ways than one.

He was prepared when he pulled into the parking lot at the police barracks and threw the car into park and shut off the engine. Aspirins hadn't helped his pounding head, and he laid it back against the headrest. Will knew that the headache he had now was just a sample of the one he would have after filing the missing persons report for Judy.

Will Kennedy was no fool. His past would raise a red flag, and the cops would be swarming around him like hornets. He cautiously climbed the stairs to Detective Swenson's office.

"He's not in yet," said the girlish officer who checked Will's license before handing him a pen and paper work. "Here, you can fill these out over there; I'll make sure Detective Swenson gets them."

On trembling legs, Will wearily returned to his car, wiped the sweat from his forehead, and threw the paperwork into the glove compartment. The furious pounding of his heart echoed in his ears.

Will's anxiety was mounting and he knew he had to keep it manageable. A good run would help. The traffic was light so he drove to South Boston and pulled in near the L Street Bathhouse. He was in luck—the tide was out.

He stretched his aching legs and back and began his run in a slow, rhythmic pace. Will felt ready to pick it up and moved away from oncoming walkers, their dogs, and kids and cut across the grass to the nearly deserted beach and scattered a dozen squawking seagulls who took to the air. He sprinted along the shoreline, around the rocks, and over the threads of dried seaweed that crunched beneath his feet.

To the regulars who pass sun-splashed mornings relaxing on the benches that line the grassy borders around Pleasure Bay, Castle Island, and Carson Beach, Will was an awesome sight. He still possessed the speed of a great sprinter, the stamina of a marathoner, and the racing heart of a Triple Crown-winning thoroughbred.

Kennedy was a nice, tight package. A few of the regulars, who winter in Florida and spend summers hanging over the rails at Suffolk Downs in East Boston smoking cigars and studying their racing forms, noted Will's running times. Before you could say "And they're off," any one of them could rattle off the post-positions and racing times of remarkable thoroughbreds, like the great Citation in '48 and the heart-stopping Secretariat in the '70s.

Will's running times were no exception, given his age. They made side bets on how fast it took him to get from, say, the blue trash barrel over there to the first brick building on Carson Beach. The football junkies kept a record of all of the state's mile-long races, the winners and their times, and compared them to Will's.

Some of them were professional handicappers, retired lawyers, politicians, plumbers, and cops who recalled placing their gaming bets with Will years ago when he was sober enough to tend bar at the Perkins Pub.

Fitzy crushed his cigarette on the ground. "Boy, Kennedy cleaned up his act. What a pain in the ass he was when he was pill popping and drinking. Hey, did you guys read that article in Sunday's paper about Bob Hayes? He was always Kennedy's hero and still is." He fished the clipping from his shirt pocket. "I cut this article out for him in case he missed it."

Karl Kapinski took the last draw from his cigar. "The article was okay; Frankel could have added to it, but he talked more about the time Bob Hayes spent with Landry and the Dallas Cowboys and his drinking and drugs than he did about Bob Hayes the Olympian. Too bad the booze wrecked Bullet's liver and kidneys, the poor bastard. It killed him."

"Bullet" Bob Hayes held the unofficial title of "The Fastest Human Alive." He distinguished himself as a sports great by being the only athlete ever to win an Olympic Gold Medal and a Super Bowl Ring. During the 1964 Summer Olympics in Tokyo, the fleet-footed sprinter blew past his competitors and shattered the record books for the 100 meter in a screaming 10.6 seconds, running in borrowed track shoes on a chewed-up track. Bullet's illustrious career was capped with induction into the Football Hall of Fame, but he didn't live long enough to savor the honor.

What Will Kennedy savored were the occasional handshakes and good-natured back slaps from his armchair audience. It was good enough for him. As they followed his form along the shoreline, their trained eyes knew he was struggling, probably with his right hip. His stride was off, his right leg nearly dragging.

He turned his face from the glare of the sun and shivered from the piercing cries of the circling gulls. Sweat trickled from his forehead and down his neck. His jersey was soaked. Waves of nausea washed over him, and his legs felt like jelly. Will slowed and methodically limped toward the bathhouse for a hot shower.

A glint from the bronze statue of Father Joseph LaPorte caught his eye and he drew close to it and nearly collapsed on a nearby bench. Will reflected on the monument raised by the community in honor of the dead priest, whose hands were eternally placed on the shoulders of a youngster. It was a decent and moral likeness commemorating everything LaPorte had done for the good kids and the troubled kids like himself, the true sons of South Boston and proud of it.

Father Joe had died too young and soon for screw-ups like Will, whose ministry covered back streets, dark alleys, housing projects, holding cells, schoolyards, and the beaches of South Boston. Father Joe had taken it to the streets, the same streets that led Will to this day and time and that had merged his life with Judy Lydon's so many years ago.

On sizzling summer nights when the humidity ran as high as a young man's sex drive, Will and his buddies sprawled on the soft grasses of Thomas Park, behind the monument or bushes feeling up their girls and guzzling beer.

Out of the darkness Father Joe's stately figure appeared, and he'd listen to their confessions under the cloak of the ink-blue sky, the light of the moon, and gleaming stars that seemed within reach from atop the knoll on Thomas Park.

One could see forever from that hill, high above the sloping streets and rooftops of the triple-deckers of South Boston to the shimmering skyline in the distance. Twinkling lights glittered like sequins and marked the windows of high-rise buildings that soared above the headlights and red tail-lights of cars coming or going. Streetlights guided travelers on the roads and illuminated the dark waters, boats, and shipping vessels docked along the waterfront of Boston Harbor.

Today, no such light guided Will. Judy was missing. He was an anxious traveler on a dark, treacherous road. His hands dropped to his thighs, and he rubbed them slowly, back and forth, endlessly. He lowered his head between his knees and stared at the ground, thinking of the days when he had moved numbly through life in an alcohol-induced, screw-yourself fog: a gun-toting, pot-smoking, pill-popping punk who spent most of his time sitting slouched on a court house bench.

Will recalled Judge Callahan glancing over a pile of documents that bore his name, then, looking down at him over glasses perched on his long, sliver of a nose. "Mr. Kennedy, you've got quite a record. I have a roster here of your offensive and destructive extracurricular activities. You seem to enjoy holding people up at gunpoint, assaulting police officers, and barroom brawling.

"You've been booking numbers and have been on probation twice in the past four years. You and your cohorts were at Flannigan's the night a Mr. Joseph Riley was sent to the hospital with a concussion and severed ear. One of you belted him with a beer bottle, but surprisingly there were no witnesses. Do you know anything about it?"

Will remembered staring up at him with a smirk on his face.

The judge had returned the smirk and cleared his throat. "I didn't think you'd remember anything about it, Mr. Kennedy." Then, as casually as sticking a stamp on an envelope, the judge gathered his paperwork, tapped it together on his oak bench, and said, "Mr. Kennedy, you seem to be a one-man crime wave, and I'm going to put a stop to it."

Will spent the next two years locked behind the gray, cinderblock walls and iron bars of the antiquated Charles Street Jail. When the day that set him free arrived, Will Kennedy was a changed man.

He had known what to do to live a good life and focused on it. He planned to get a steady job, save some money, and start a business. Christine Sandonato would be there with him; he needed her love so much he could taste it. Will knew she loved him, believed in him, and would forgive all the hurtful, stupid things he had done to her and everyone else. He vowed that she would never regret spending the rest of her life with him. Eventually, her parents would come around.

Will made a cup of hot tea, sat at the kitchen table, and wrote Christine a letter, a straight from the heart letter. Expressions of his love and devotion gushed like some meandering mountain stream turned mighty river, a spring thaw in his soul that flowed through his fingertips. He carefully folded into an envelope his words of love and plans for the future and slipped the letter into the mailbox at the end of the street near Cabot's Drug Store.

Will waited for Christine's answer, eager to hear the quick, lightness of her step on the front stairs or the lyrical sound of her voice and laughter on the phone, but she never called and she never came. Judy Lydon did.

He never dreamed his life would be as messed up now as it was then. What he did know was that the cops would be gunning for him for the disappearance of Judy.

Outside the bathhouse, Will heaved a heavy sigh and looked at the sky. A cotton-ball like cloud drifted across the bright, blue heavens. Gusting wind carried the cloud higher until it vanished.

Will dropped his head in his hands and massaged his temples. His headache was worse. A sickening nausea filled his gut.

He sat on that hard bench hidden between the statue of Father La Porte and a sprawling maple tree until the late afternoon sun moved across his body and cast a long, grotesque shadow of himself over the ground beneath him. He emerged from his cover and began the slow, painful walk back to the bathhouse, past the benches left vacant by people hurrying home to bathe their babies, start dinner, or watch the evening news.

A deep, crusty voice called out to him; "Hey, buddy, how 'ya doing? It's been a long time."

Will tried to place the ravaged face and debilitated form before him, and then it came to him. *God Almighty, its Glenn Kelly!*

CHAPTER SIX

J udy Lyndon's life had changed forever the night Father
LaPorte escorted her and her drunken girlfriends from
Thomas Park to her house. She had confessed to him that
she was pregnant with Glenn Kelly's baby and now had to
tell her mother. She had been trouble to her parents for years.

Glenn and his family held the all-time record in South
Boston for what the locals called "scumbags." They were
feared and loathed, and for good reasons. Glenn had begun
a twenty-to twentyfive-year stretch at Walpole for attempted
murder and parole violations. He had shot out his girlfriend's
eye, had meant to kill her - shoot her in the head - but his
drunken aim was off, and she had lived to tell about it.

Glenn was also dating Judy on the side.

She hampered the investigation into the beating death
of Glenn's elderly landlord, who had timidly confronted him
and his brothers over their misuse of a parking space, by
boldly professing a false alibi on their behalf.

Glenn's mother had finally been convicted of grand lar-
ceny and was serving time in Framingham. The neighborhood rejoiced at Glenn's sentencing and then exploded in
outright glee when the evening news reported that his father

and brother had been shot dead in Medford during a bank robbery run amuck.

Howie Marr of the *Traveler's Post* put his own brand of wit and sarcasm on the comedy of errors and misadventures of the Kelly Family and wrote, "Sweet dreams, Glenn; those bunks are hard as rocks, and did I mention night visitors? Oh, and Glen, don't bend over if you drop the soap."

Father LaPorte hoped Glenn's bad-boy image had attracted Judy to him and not the same devilish blood running through her veins. In the Lydon's living room, the kind priest kneeled and prayed for forgiveness of Judy's sin and strength, and faith for her mother. He prayed for the health and holiness of the child and asked God to deliver them from evil.

Judy's mother sent her to St. Theresa's Home for Wayward Girls somewhere in the mid-west where she gave birth to Glenn Kelly's child. She held the infant once before Sister Anne efficiently whisked the newborn to the eager arms of a childless naval officer and his wife.

Judy returned home a week later and spent the next year depressed and anxious, sleeping during the day and wandering with her friends at night. She rarely spoke to her mother.

Mrs. Lydon wondered what her husband would have thought of their daughter now, not that it mattered because he was dead and she had been glad of it. She knew he would have defended Judy, who was just like him: a violent bully, raving liar, thief, and a cheat.

His unshakeable defense of Judy's actions had caused a fiery rift in their marriage, and Judy had feverishly fanned the smoldering coals of resentment between them. They snubbed the petite and lovely Mrs. Lydon and scorned her in her own home.

Judy was neither petite nor lovely. Rather, she appeared big, beefy, and average looking, had a poor complexion, and when not angry or sulking, her smile revealed a distinct space between her front teeth. Judy's crowning glory was a head of thick red hair that fell around her squat face. She looked just like her father.

Mrs. Lydon prayed for a sign that Judy would change. The months passed, and one hot, summer evening, she watched from the window as Judy sat with Will Kennedy, drinking at the bottom of Thomas Park. She was never far from his side after that night.

She thanked Jesus Christ and the Virgin Mother that Will had not been in jail for well over a year. He came from good enough stock, hard-working, sober, law-abiding people, but he was the black sheep of the family.

The Kennedys were all good-natured, round faced, blond haired, and blue eyed, but not Will. Mrs. Lydon had read somewhere that years ago, the Spaniards ravaged the shores of Ireland and changed the face of Ireland's history. She wondered if Will's looks were the mark of some horrible raping of an Irish girl by a mysterious, shadowy foreigner, which would account for his dark, brooding looks.

With nearly black hair and eyes of an odd, light green that sparkled and shined like tiny jewels, Will's good looks were intriguing. A bluish-green five o'clock shadow permanently marked his beard line, and his smooth, swarthy complexion stretched across a handsome face that boasted superb bone structure.

His cheekbones supported a classic aquiline nose, which was a bit too long, a splinter's width too deep at its bridge but enough to make it interesting and imperfect and Will ruggedly handsome. He was quiet and shy and seemed uncomfortable with himself, although he loosened up pretty good after a few hours of drinking with his pals.

When the weather was warm and the ground dry, they sat around the white marble monument atop Thomas Park, behind the high school, laughing, drinking, and giving the finger to the kids in class who dared to peek out the windows. When the cold weather came or it rained, the gang moved their perpetual celebration into a dark hallway or the cold, dank cellar of some vacant, rat-infested building and played poker or gin. Life was good for Judy, Will, and the drunken delinquents they hung out with.

Mrs. Lydon was sure that Will had potential for something or someone, at some time. She prayed it was not for her someone, her daughter, at this time. It would come to no good.

CHAPTER SEVEN

Will recalled Mrs. Lydon's stony silence when Judy announced she was pregnant. This time it was his baby. He remembered hanging his head to avoid her icy stare and could still hear her strained voice quivering.

"You two are nothing but trouble - a couple of irresponsible, delinquents! I don't know how you're going to bring up a child. Neither of you has ever graduated from high school or ever held a respectable job!"

Her blue eyes blazed with fury and disgust, as she turned to Will. "You have no money, no job, and a criminal record, and you're only twenty-two years old. You should be ashamed of yourself. You're nothing but a bum!

"And you," she spewed to Judy, "have had every opportunity handed to you on a silver platter. And what do you do, you lie, cheat, steal, sneak, drink, and get yourself pregnant, not once, but twice with hoodlums who don't care for you! You're only seventeen and can barely take care of yourself, never mind a baby. The only thing that you two have in common is trouble. May God help us!" she moaned and sat wiping on the hem of her apron the tears from her eyes.

Thinking back, Will supposed what attracted him and Judy to each other in the first place, was trouble and a need for acceptance they found only in each other. Together they made sense of it all and fell in love because of it.

Jamie was born two months later, and Will and Judy married a few weeks thereafter. They set up housekeeping on the first floor of her mother's house, just a stone's throw away from Thomas Park. Will eased up on his drinking and worked the loading docks, so there was money coming in.

Their newfound existence was like paradise. After regular Sunday dinners with Mrs. Lydon, they tucked Jamie in a carriage and strolled up the hills and down the streets near the park, crossed the boulevard, and walked the crescent shoreline of Dorchester Bay and Castle Island.

They waved to neighbors across the street and stopped to speak with friends who peered in to see Jamie. Their well-wishers smiled and shook their hands in congratulations. It was a storybook ending for Will, Judy, Mrs. Lydon, and the baby.

Jamie was barely three months old, tucked in for the night, and fast asleep when Judy finished wrapping a gift and left for a baby shower. Will sat on the front porch with his legs propped on the front railing and was having a few beers with Stevie B., more aware of the clean scent of the summer night's coming storm than their conversation.

The day's oppressive heat and humidity had carried from the bay a sheet of heavy fog that had drifted ashore and cloaked the figures of kids passing and muffled their voices. The click-clacking sound of their footsteps trailed and was lost in the booms of rolling thunder that seemed to echo for miles. Mellow glows of lightning followed and flashed above the horizon over the bay. The temperature dropped and the wind picked up; the storm was near.

Will went inside for refills, to close the windows, and check on Jamie. Stevie B. said that he would always remember Will's sudden wail and the image of his hugging that little baby to his chest. Jamie Kennedy was buried at Mount Wollaston Cemetery in Quincy, alongside Judy's father.

Over time, Will's denial, anger, bargaining, and sorrow gave way to acceptance and understanding. Judy never reached that stage in her grief; it stalled in a searing anger that engulfed every aspect of her being and torched those around her. It seeped into all she had become and dredged up all she had buried of an ugly past, and she embraced it.

Will became her primary target, so he took up running, as far away from her rage as his legs would carry him. He stopped drinking too, and his emotional life without Judy and booze, elevated his spirit to some higher plane he never knew existed. His newfound peace inflamed her burning resentment toward him.

Judy Lydon Kennedy became a walking time bomb, whitewashed under a cover of efficiency, drive, and a pleasant smile.

To the senior management at the Quincy Quarry Bank and Trust Company in Quincy, Massachusetts, Judy appeared to be an ideal employee. However, when a flood of complaints first poured in, she and a few bank employees scrambled to the safety of higher ground but never made it.

CHAPTER EIGHT

Gravel crunching beneath the weight of a steady stream of cars, trucks, and foot traffic leading to Richie's Marina during boating season is probably too mundane a sound for the hundred or so sea lovers who moor their boats and yachts there to think about when the languid days and clear blue skies of summer call them to take to the sea.

They load the arms and backs of their wives and parents, kids and friends with life vests, coolers, potato chips, beer, fishing rods, and bait, and herd them across the graveled lot, along the swaying footpaths, over the creaking piers, and to the bays that moor their prides of the sea. Their boats bob and weave in the wakes of the outgoing vessels and turns of the tide and bear names, like *Thank You Judge Stein*, *Paula Lee and Me*, *Steve's Sea-Saw*, and *Beer with Us*.

Sweede's *Grey Ghost* sat high and dry above the hustle and bustle, its engine housing void of the twin Mercs that had propelled him and his buddies to Stellwagen when their trip ended in a cloud of black smoke. The sea strainer was gone, too, yanked from the Bayliner to Richie Kenney's Marine Shop.

Richie was the best marine mechanic around, and his shop sat a hundred feet away from where the *Grey Ghost* sat dry-docked. Richie scrutinized every mechanism of the engines and sea strainer, and then called Sweede.

It wasn't long before he heard the crush of gravel and slam of car doors. Sweede and Ted made their way into the shop, where Richie awaited them. "I've got something to show you that I found in your boat's sea strainer." He positioned his tweezers over the strainer, carefully lifted out a tangled mess of debris, and dangled it before their eyes.

The detectives stepped forward. Ted put on his glasses, and Sweede pressed closer. "What the hell is that?"

"It's hair! The whole strainer is packed with it. Take a look at this!"

Sweede squinted. Thousands of strands of reddish hair and crumb-sized bits of head tissue and bone fragments matted the sea strainer. Ted stepped back and whistled, but Sweede only stared at the strainer. "Oh shit!"

Richie dropped the tweezers on a paper towel. "That was your problem. The hair and that other stuff blocked sea water from passing through the strainer and up to cool the engines. Didn't you notice the temperature rising on the thermostat? The warning system must have been flashing and buzzing off the charts!"

Sweede cleared his throat and ran his hands through his hair. "No, either the circuit blew or it wasn't hooked up right." He sighed heavily and rubbed his palm over his mouth. "I don't know what the hell happened to it."

As Ted called headquarters, Sweede waited. Twenty minutes later, Richie's shop buzzed like a skill saw with detectives and forensics. They cordoned the building while technicians bagged and boxed the evidence before leaving.

Sweede and Ted finished some paper work and made their way across the parking lot to White Finn's for a beer. The crunch of gravel held no pleasant memories for Sweede. He felt its heat through the soles of his shoes, and the sun's burning rays seared the back of his neck.

He was so damn hot and tired. "Why the hell does this crap always happen on Friday afternoons? We're covering for vacations; we might have to work all damn weekend!"

Ted agreed. "I'm going to miss my grandson's birthday party." He opened the door for Sweede, and they stepped from the glare of the sun and its blistering heat into the cool, quiet, sanctum of an empty bar.

While Ted loosened his tie, released his collar button, and ordered a Bud Lite and cheeseburger, Sweede scanned the menu. "Give me a Sam Adams on tap and steak tips."

The bartender shook his head. "Sorry, we're out; no Sam on tap until the morning."

Ted snickered and threw back a cold mouthful of beer.

Sweede caught Ted's grin and decided to go with the flow. "Well, give me a Bass on tap."

The bartender blinked a few times, opened his mouth to speak, paused, and then cleared his throat. "We're out. The delivery truck broke down, but it should be here any minute."

Ted lifted the glass to his mouth; it stifled the sound of his chuckling.

Sweede glanced at him and the empty bar. He yanked off his neck tie, stuffed it in the pocket of his sport coat, peeled it off, and threw it on the chair beside him. He unbuttoned his collar, rolled up his sleeves, and glared at the bartender. "What do you have on tap?"

The bartender stepped back. "We, we have Sea Glass. It's a micro-brew made in Hull. The hops are imported from Germany."

Sweede scowled. "Who the hell drinks that shit? A bunch of broads?"

Ted let out a good belly laugh. "I wouldn't say that in front of Captain Chung, if I were you. He and his wife drink it because their son and daughter-in-law brew it!"

Sweede shook his head. "It fucking figures, give me a Miller Lite."

"You've got it, sir."

The first taste of ice-cold beer washed over Sweede's parched tongue when he felt a vibration on his right flank. He lay the glass down with a thud.

Ted picked his up, drained it, and motioned to the bartender. "I'll have another."

Sweede read the message, hung up, sat back, and cut into his steak tips.

Ted swallowed and wiped his mouth. "What's going on?"

Before answering, Sweede finished his beer. "A guy and his kid found a hand caught in the netting of their lobster trap down in Scituate. They think it might be related to the disappearance of Will Kennedy's wife. A wedding band with their initials engraved on it is still on the finger."

"What time are we meeting with Kennedy?"

Sweede raked his fingers through his graying hair. "Won't know until the captain calls back." He could see the marina and the pleasure boats swaying gently with the incoming tide, their owners laughing and lounging on the decks. "What a time to have my boat screwed up! I should have stayed in the navy."

CHAPTER NINE

With staunch expertise, Henry Nunn had navigated the seven seas. He commanded the crew of his destroyer with a cool excellence first exhibited in Vietnam with his river boat, the same distinction that moved him up in rank to commander in short order - just under ten years.

Nunn was bred for military service. As a third-generation graduate of the U.S. Naval Academy, he epitomized the very best in officer training: structured, self-directed, resourceful, patriotic, brave, commanding, and diplomatic when it counted.

Henry deployed to Vietnam on his fifth wedding anniversary; his wife, Adele, joined the Red Cross and landed in Vietnam a few months later. The thirty-four-year-old warrior spent the next year of his life overseeing his crew of gunners. They patrolled the weed-choked, mosquito-infested waterways of the Mekong Delta in thirty-two-foot fiberglass riverboats, searching for Viet Cong-intended weapons shipments.

As masters of camouflage, the Viet Cong disguised themselves as smiling, conical-hatted peasants plying boats laden with gunpowder and rifles hidden beneath mounds of rice. In the tops of the mangroves high above the riverboats, they hid with machine guns or crouched with rifles in the trackless mud of the elephant grass.

Still, the Viet Cong could not hide themselves or their weapon shipments from Nunn and his team, who had become stealthy and skillful at their jobs. They would sniff them out and track them down.

Word was that Nunn used his rifle as much as the gunners did their grenade launchers and roundabout machine guns. The navy recognized their efforts with field promotions and honors, but Nunn downplayed all of it by calling himself Captain Blanks.

Despite the validations the U.S. Navy bestowed upon him and an ornate collage of brightly colored medals, stripes, and ribbons, Henry dwelled on a glaring failure: he may have shot his rifle with deadly accuracy, but, in the bedroom fired blanks.

When he and Adele returned to the States, they took matters into their own capable hands and contacted adoption agencies. A letter arrived one sunny Saturday morning when the two sat sipping coffee and reading the paper on the patio. They packed their bags in a flash and returned home the next evening with a newborn infant, whom they named Frederick - Freddy for short - after Henry's father.

The family moved with the commander's transfers to Pascagoula, Mississippi, San Diego, Groton, Connecticut, and, finally, historic Quincy, Massachusetts, where they settled down for good.

They bought a big colonial up the street from the naval base in Squantum, across from a woodsy thicket and where an osprey's nest sits atop a pole and marks the beginning of a quarter mile or so of marshland that extends into Quincy

Bay. Adele named their home, BayMist, and it was a land-mark of sorts to marine travelers, who admired it from their boats.

It sat as solid as the granite coastline, high on a hillside. Its backyard sloped a good hundred feet, where it stretched into Quincy Bay. Sturdy Doric columns supported the red slate roof of a wraparound porch and second floor. A widow's walk surrounded the third floor. Henry and Adele heightened the effect with a massive weather vane, a copper schooner under full sail atop a white cupola. They undertook no project halfheartedly, including the rearing of their son.

Their devotion to Freddy was unparalleled by all who knew them, and the ocean and the military bound the fam-ily in camaraderie. Henry taught his son to sail, and, on any given day, Adele and Freddy would climb the narrow stairs to the attic - Freddy's look-out - and step onto the widow's walk. Freddy became a student of the land and sea far below his perch.

He would adjust his binoculars and scan the waters and the marshland to the south, then moved to the north side of the widow's walk where he turned his attention to the Boston skyline.

The ritual ended when the Dorchester Heights Memo-rial, which sits at the peak of Thomas Park in South Bos-ton, came into focus and where Freddy became one with the soldiers there in 1776, commanding his troops to fire their cannons on the British forces below.

Freddy became Brigadier General John Thomas, who according to Boston lore was General George Washing-ton's right hand man. Henry and Adele decorated their son's look-out with Revolutionary War memorabilia. Illustrations of soldiers and rifles hung on the walls above hundreds of models of cannons and ships, swords and tin soldiers, and horses hitched to wooden wagons.

The room was Freddy's world, his own pseudo armed asylum that took him far away from his bed-wetting, poor school grades, and absence of athletic ability. He cried in a dark corner of that lookout when Henry died and punched the walls after Adele's accountant said that money was so tight that Freddy needed a job.

He was hired as a custodian at the Quincy Quarry Bank and Trust, promoted to the stock room a few years later, never earned another upgrade, and became something of a curiosity. Freddy waved in everyone's face his autographed photos of Suzanne Sommers, openly wept when telling them he had refused a scholarship to Harvard to care for his ailing mother's estate, and displayed a lock of Bigfoot's fur in a plastic bag pinned to his jeans.

Freddy bragged that a squirrel or bird could be dropped with one hit of a BB - a rabbit, two. He claimed to be a direct descendent of George Washington and flashed pictures of his inheritance - a hundred acres of Mount Vernon farmland he was leasing to the CIA for underground and covert operations he could not discuss.

Freddy's embellishments and make-believes were matched only by his colleague - Judy Lydon Kennedy. Her stories were less fanciful, more believable, dangerously devious, and proved to be her downfall.

CHAPTER TEN

Sweede and Ted sat in Captain Chung's wheat-colored office at the state police barracks reading reports and studying photos. Chung peeled the wrapper off a brownie and sat sipping his tea.

Sweede whistled softly, shook his head, and handed the photos to Ted. "Christ, no wonder that kid threw up; she saw the hand."

Chung swallowed and wiped his mouth. "Saw it - she tried to untangle it from the trap. It was caught on the netting! It was dusk; she thought it was a baby lobster!"

Sweede looked over the file and read aloud. "'Olivia Aruda, age eight, Tilden Street, Scituate - out pulling legal lobster traps with her father, Emmanuel Aruda, age thirty-one.'"

Chung finished his tea and dropped the spoon into the mug. "The kid's having nightmares; her father's not much better."

Sweede flipped the page, read the report, and compared it again to the photographs: a nine by twelve picture of a female's bloated left hand, severed below the palm, a couple of artificial nails still intact, and a wedding band in place on the ring finger. Sweede closed the report and slid it across Chung's desk who laid it aside.

"You two get over there and break the news to her husband. Ask him to come in and identify the ring. Oh, and see if there's a hair brush that we can take a few samples from. We're looking for a DNA match. Then get over to the bank where she worked and see what they have to say."

As the detectives were about to leave, Chung added, "And by the way, Sweede, there's more than a good chance Judy Kennedy was out at Stellwagen with you - riding in your boat's clogged sea strainer."

Sweede turned and looked at the grin on Chung's face. "What do you mean?"

"What I mean is, we're going to see if the DNA from the hand and hairbrush samples match the matted hair and scalp pieces that clogged your sea strainer." He chuckled. "I bet Judy Kennedy screwed up the engines on your boat!"

Sweede slammed the door on Chung and turned to Ted. "What are the fucking odds of that happening? I won't fucking believe it until I have the fucking proof. It's too much of a fucking coincidence!"

Ted grabbed his jacket. "We'll see if you have your fucking proof in about hour. Let's get to Will Kennedy's house."

Will handed over the hairbrush to the detectives, but knew in all probability that Judy was dead. He agreed to view the ring but knew it was just a formality. The photographs of her jewelry and the inscription on the wedding band were proof enough. He tried to listen to the detectives, but their voices seemed to echo and didn't make much sense. The air in the room seemed suffocating and heavy on his chest, strangling the words in his throat. Will resisted the urge to run from that stifling room and gripped the armrests of the chair, slowly and cautiously answering their questions in a voice that seemed to resonate from someone else in some faraway place.

When the detectives left, Will iced a washcloth, pressed it firmly across his aching forehead, and lay down. Judy's time was over. He would never hear her voice again. No screaming or accusations, no forced conversations. Her life had ended most likely as she had lived: violently, in some snarled web of deceit. She had made someone else's life a living hell and paid for it with her own. Will was not naive. He was and always would be street smart, a true son of South Boston. He knew the drill. The hell he suffered as Judy's husband would not end with her death. The detectives would be back.

CHAPTER ELEVEN

Alfred Locke sat in a corner office of the Quincy Quarry Bank and Trust dictating a memo regarding the bank's contribution to its employees' dental plan when the detectives were quietly ushered into his office. He rose, fastened the buttons of his suit coat over his ample belly, and extended a hearty handshake. "Please sit down. I assume you're here regarding Judy Kennedy. We're greatly disturbed by her absence."

"It's more than an absence, Mr. Locke," Sweede said.

"It's Alfred; call me Alfred."

Sweede continued. "Alfred, we have good reason to believe that Judy is dead."

Locke raised his eyebrows. "Dead?"

"That's right, dead. Her husband just identified her wedding band, and we'll have conclusive evidence after DNA testing."

"DNA testing?"

Sweede nodded matter-of-factly. "Yes. We can't go into detail yet because we're just gathering information. You know what I mean."

Locke glanced down, smoothed his tie, and then flashed a brief, anxious smile at Sweede. "Of course, of course I do;

well, uh, what can I tell you? We're always ready to cooperate with law enforcement."

Alfred Locke was not a man who expressed himself easily. He shifted in his chair, as though in great distress, and cleared his throat. "May I, uh, that is, is it proper for me to ask how she died?"

Ted shook his head. "We're not quite sure yet. How long has she worked here?"

Locke pulled up her work history. "Judy has - rather, Judy worked here for a little over twenty years."

"What did she do?"

Locke loosened his tie. "She opened new accounts."

Sweede interrupted. "Opened new accounts? Was she a manager?"

"No, no, she was not."

"You mean she worked here for over twenty years and never made management? Isn't that a little unusual?"

Locke dusted a speck of unseen lint from his sleeve. "Well, ah, yes, one could assume so."

Ted's voice softened. "Alfred, was there a problem with Judy?"

"I don't care to speak ill of the dead, detective, but I, rather we - the board - felt that she had issues that were less favorable, issues not conducive, that is, that would not lend themselves to a, rather, the standard of professionalism normally associated with bank employees, much less one entrusted with a management position."

"We know this is difficult for you, but could you be more specific?"

Alfred unbuttoned his suit jacket and settled back in the well-cushioned chair. "Frankly, I've been looking for a reason to fire her for years, but she's efficient, shows up, has a decent rapport with customers, and rarely makes a mistake."

Ted waited a moment before continuing. "I sense a 'but' coming. Go on."

Alfred removed his glasses, laid them on his desk, and leaned toward the investigators.

"Look, Judy was something of a screwball, maybe a bit unbalanced. A few years ago, there was an opening in our investment division. She wanted the job but wasn't qualified. Didn't have the education, experience, you know, couldn't see the big picture or carry over information."

Sweede made a notation in his notebook. "Alfred, give us an example."

"All right, let's say half of the West Coast falls into the ocean; one would invest in transportation, building supplies, healthcare, food suppliers, energy - anything needed to get the state up and running again. She just couldn't connect all the dots.

"In fact, while she waited for our decision, our share prices just happened to fall by four cents. Judy called in sick for three days and blamed it on the falling stock prices. I guess that she was trying to prove in her own way how committed she was to the welfare of the bank."

"Anything else you'd like to tell us, Alfred?" Sweede inquired.

"Yes, as a matter of fact, there is. Other than the fact that she continually undermined senior management with her criticism and demeaned our positions and job performance behind our backs, there is something else.

"I never trusted her. In fact, I was recently notified of a $1.5 million discrepancy affecting a dozen or so commercial accounts. Of course, I alerted the proper authorities when the first divergence appeared, a week or so ago.

"Account complaints have been pouring in ever since. I expect the bank examiners in this week. I trust that you will keep that information confidential since we're not certain who the wrongdoer is yet, and of course, the publicity would be…"

Sweede interrupted. "We get it, Alfred. Do you suspect Judy?"

Alfred glanced down at his folded hands and hesitated. "As I said, I don't care to speak ill of the dead, but this development with Judy seems timely and ties in with another minor issue I've found troubling.

His voice rose with irritation. "Look, I play racquetball with her husband, Will, once in a while. He's a decent guy, makes a pretty good living. I don't think he and Judy got along so well. Be that as it may, a few months ago we finished up a game and went to the clubhouse for a sandwich.

"Will was talking about setting up an employees' bonus program based on job performance - like the one that the bank has. He said that the bonuses Judy earned with us were impressive and that he had no idea that she could earn an extra $100,000 a year managing commercial accounts."

Alfred shrugged his shoulders. "I didn't know what to say to him! Judy obviously lied to him about her position, and she certainly never received a bonus from us. So I did some checking. She takes out a personal loan every December and pays it off a couple of months later.

Don't know what her game was. The last loan was for $145,000."

Ted lifted his brows. "Wow! Do the Kennedys live the high life, Alfred?"

"Not by any standard that I've observed; 'modest' would be my choice of words."

He coughed and cleared his throat. "Excuse me," he said, sipping a glass of water. He swallowed and cleared his throat again. "Ah, that's better; as I was saying, not that Judy wouldn't, rather, didn't want the high life."

"Go on," said Sweede.

Locke took a deep breath. "Some months ago, she tried to cozy up with one of our junior VPs - really cozy up - if you know what I mean. Judy is, rather was, tenacious as a pit bull. As I said, she wanted to be at the top."

Sweede's eyes widened with interest. "Did it develop into anything? Was she having an affair?"

Alfred's lips tightened. "Yes, I'm afraid she was having an affair. Don't know if she still is, or rather was."

Sweede leaned forward. "Is he here? We need to talk with him."

Locke leaned his head to one side, methodically massaging his right temple. "You'll be speaking with a she, not a he. Her name is Ginger Stoolman, and she took the day off."

Sweede made a notation. "Alfred, anyone else Judy may have been close to?"

"Yes, yes, there is. His name is Freddy, rather Frederick Washington Nunn."

Ted jotted down the name.

Alfred Locke scowled. "I understand Freddy's parents on both sides were descendants of our first president, at least that's what he says."

Sweede snickered and looked away from his notes and at Alfred. "The cherry-tree-chopping George?"

"Yes. And the president who incited our right to bear arms."

CHAPTER TWELVE

Ginger Stoolman cleaned her .38 revolver, dropped it into its case, tossed it onto the passenger seat, and headed home to shower and change. She checked in the mirror the look of her naked body, admired what she saw, but resisted the urge to fondle herself. There was no time.

Ginger slid into cream-colored slacks and a black silk blouse, but left the uppermost buttons open. She yanked up her sheer red bra a bit - the one that looked best with her hooped earrings - slipped into her black stilettos, and glided to the mirrored walls of her bedroom to gaze at her reflection.

With a sip of scotch, she celebrated her appeal. Ginger was in the mood for sex, not discussion, and the more the merrier. She hoped luck was on her side and that the detectives were nothing more than a couple of sex starved, civil servants.

Stoolman scanned the room. The shrimp cocktails were strategically placed beside the autographed copy of Mailer's book on Marilyn Monroe. She sank a bottle of chardonnay into the ice bucket to the left of the book and half-closed the blinds against the glare of the afternoon's sun.

Hmm, she thought, *the detectives can face the light.*

She lit a few candles in the bedroom, straightened an abstract painting over her headboard, and turned back the sheets. Ginger returned to the living room and arranged on the bar tall, white wine glasses, then tumbled into soft, silken pillows strewn on the black couch, sipped her scotch, and waited for the detectives.

Her wait was short, and Ginger buzzed them in and sized them up.

Sweede handed her his business card, and Ted followed suit.

At the sight of Sweede, Ginger ran over her thighs her short, stubby fingers and guessed that with heels on, she was nearly as tall as he. She gazed over his body, slowly and deliberately, rested for a split second on his groin before raising her eyes to his and smiling.

Her scarlet-colored lips showed more of her gums than teeth, and the too sweet smell of her perfume hung thick in the air.

Sweede returned her unwanted gaze, yawned, and took his appointed seat. He hated sluts and could smell one a mile away.

Smiling, Ted dropped his head and flipped through the pages of his notebook.

"Could I interest you boys in a glass of scotch or wine? My brother, Mitchell, has a small vineyard in the Sonoma Valley."

Sweede declined, "Ms. Stoolman, we're on duty."

She wrenched the cork from the bottle and lit a cigarette. "You play by the rules then."

"You bet. We're here to discuss Judy Kennedy."

She rolled her eyes and smirked at Sweede. "Yes, Alfred Locke told me as much. And in case you're wondering, I play by the rules too - that is, most of the time."

He tilted his head and signaled his partner.

Ted picked it up. "That's not exactly what we've heard, Ms. Stoolman. It's our understanding that you and Judy Kennedy were pretty chummy in and out of work."

Ginger raised her glass and lowered her voice. "I'm a curious, universal woman. That's all."

Ted studied her for a moment. "You don't seem like the typical banking type to me. Don't bank executives wear gray suits and act a little more conservative than you?"

"I told you, I'm a universal type, I really do see the big picture, and I'm an investment whiz! I wear traditional clothing and act conservative when it counts. And I can adapt to any situation. I'm a pretty good actress too! Oh, look what I've done, wine all over my blouse. Anyone have a handkerchief?"

The detectives exchanged glances.

Ginger lifted a napkin and dabbed slowly and precisely at the stained blouse that clung to her breast. She released a few buttons, shook out the napkin, and caressed and stroked it against her flimsy bra.

Sweede folded his arms across his chest.

Ted watched her impatiently. "Ms. Stoolman, Ginger, may I call you Ginger?"

She looked down at her cleavage and up at Ted. "Yes, if it serves to make you more comfortable."

"Ginger, it's been brought to our attention that you and Mrs. Kennedy shared a friendship that was probably based on her desire to move up in the ranks."

"Well now, detective, that sounds nearly correct; however, we're not on a ship or in the military. The word or phrase you should be using is corporate ladder, 'moving up the corporate ladder.'

"And to answer your question, Judy would do just about anything for a little prestige. Befriending me would be, without a doubt, a coup for a substandard such as Judy." Ginger stretched her arms over her head and shook and tousled her hair. "It's unfortunate she couldn't face reality or finality."

"Let's talk more about that, Ginger," Ted pressed.

"All right, let's talk more about that. Judy lacked any real intellect; she had a basic understanding of a lot of things, but nothing beyond that. Her knowledge base was superficial at best, and she was as dull as dirt. To be perfectly clear, detective, the word, simple, would be too kind an adjective to describe her intellect.

"She may have suffered from last year's disorder of the day, you know, ADD. On the other hand, she was very devious. Go figure. All things considered, she just couldn't make the grade. She was really quite bitter about her lot in life, but it was always someone else's fault.

"Really, after all those years as a clerk, did she really think befriending me would advance her career, if that's what one would call a clerk's job, a career?"

Ted spoke quickly. "Speaking of advances, what type of advancement or advantage did the friendship offer you?"

"I was bored."

She smiled, took a sip of wine, and turned her hazy, gray eyes to Sweede. "Have you ever been bored Detective Swenson?"

Ted cut in. "Are you sure that's all it was on your part, boredom?"

Ginger cackled. "Actually, I enjoyed the chase, as I usually do."

"I thought she wasn't your type?"

Ginger took a long drag from her cigarette and blew the smoke toward his face.

"She wasn't, but like I said, I was bored. Any port in a storm, you know how it goes."

Sweede sat back and made a notation. "Yeah, I know how it goes, it depends on what's available at the port - you know, what's being imported or exported - to and from who, or should I say whom?"

"How tawdry of you, Detective Swenson. I get your meaning and have heard it all before," she hissed.

Ted tapped his pen against his knee. "Ginger, did you ever get the feeling she wanted information from you that would advance more than her career - that would line her pocketbook maybe?"

Ginger cocked her head. "Of course I did, but, as I mentioned earlier, I play by the rules."

"You never gave her any inside information that she wasn't privy to - bank related information that would fatten her wallet?"

Ginger slapped her knee and snickered. "Of course not. I liked seeing her panting at my feet like a dog waiting for a bone."

Sweede leaned back in his chair. "When did you and Fido part company?"

She nibbled on a shrimp, and cocked her head slightly; "Hmm, let's see. I'd just returned from Geneva. I was skiing the Alps. Have you ever been, Detective Swenson?"

He ignored her question.

"I'll assume that's a no. Too bad, Geneva is simply the most..."

"Just answer the question."

"Hmmm, let's see," she said, licking her fingers. "I returned from Geneva on August 19th, and Judy and I broke up on my birthday, on August 23rd."

"Was it mutual?"

"Give me a break, of course not! Judy was livid! But my boredom had passed, and I told her as much. A few days later, I found certain items missing from my home, intimate items, photographs with certain friends. A week later, my impeccable reputation at the bank was in shambles."

Ted glanced from his notes. "You mean, that loose lips sink ships?"

Her face reddened. "I've told you once, detective, and I will not say this again: there's no need for macho sarcasm, and you can skip the military guff. I won't tolerate tawdry remarks. I've heard it all before. Got it?"

Ted uttered a counterfeit contrition. "Yes, Ginger, I do. I apologize. It's been a long day."

"Good. As I was about to say, and in answer to your question, Judy's actions had a grave effect on my career. I was up for a senior VP position and was passed over. Judy circulated a rumor that I had made unreasonable requests and unwanted sexual advances toward her, when in fact it was mutual.

"Anyway, photographs of me engaged in unorthodox sex with others were sent to board members."

She caught the detectives exchanging glances, lowered her voice, and grinned. "The good news was that, since Judy's reputation was questionable, they overlooked, as they should have, my sexual encounters. The bad news was my application for the position was turned down. They hired a home boy with ties to the community."

"I'd be pretty pissed," Ted offered.

Her face hardened like a stone, then quickly softened. She sighed, reclined, and dragged her cigarette. "I'm not the type of person who holds a grudge."

For some time, Ted studied her. "Your benevolent acceptance of being screwed is impressive. What did it cost you?"

"Detective, the cost to me was $200,000 in salary and stock options for one year, all for a garden variety piece of ass."

Sweede spoke up. "You know she's been missing, and we have reason to believe she's dead."

Ginger finished her wine. "Boo-hoo. Any more questions?"

"As a matter of fact, yes. I was just waiting for your moment of overwhelming grief to pass. When was the last time you saw or spoke with Judy?"

"I'm not sure, maybe a week or two ago. I had to walk past her to get to my safe deposit box. I really don't remember and had no reason to keep track. My office is on the top floor, and she sat in a cubicle in the main lobby. Tell me, how did that little simpleton die? Was she murdered? Did Will finally catch on, have enough of her, and snap? Did he choke the shit out of her?"

"We're just beginning the investigation. What do you know about Judy's relationship with her husband?"

She adjusted the pillow behind her back, refilled her glass, and lit another cigarette. "Nothing really. He's pretty hot looking and not the pretty-boy type either. Will is really rugged looking and has dreamy green eyes. It's a mystery to me what he saw in her. He must be as needy as she was or just naïve or maybe they were co-dependent. You know how that old saying goes, 'birds of a feather flock together.'"

"Birds of a feather, huh? You and Judy didn't mind nesting."

"Knock it off, detective. Your wise cracks are so very average. And if you're thinking about charging Will with Judy's murder, forget about it. Go sniff up another tree. I'm giving you the big picture, as I saw it.

"Really, Judy was out day and night, extorting money from people, making up job titles for herself, ruining careers, making accusations about Will trying to kill her. She was an insecure martyr who spent most of her time trying to cover it up by pretending she was smarter than everyone else.

"Her self-perception was grossly skewed. It's too bad Will never saw her for what she really was. Maybe he knew but just didn't care anymore, or it could be that he was just lazy about moving on.

"Will's a sleeper, you know, one of those guys that are really sexy, have their act together, but don't know it, don't strut their stuff. Too bad he didn't have a little more confidence in himself. I don't think he made a move without her say so.

"It worked for Judy, she had the power! He was afraid of her."

Ted looked at her thoughtfully. "You seem to know a lot about him."

"He reminds me of my brother - same type. A real good guy, funny, sensitive, and not the pretty boy type, but he's got the look. His wife's a controlling, insecure witch, just like Judy, and he's as insecure as she is.

"He's petrified of her - afraid he'll lose everything he worked for. It's a shame. And by the way, I'm sure you'll be speaking with Will frequently. Please extend my condolences to him. Let him know that I'm here, if he needs a shoulder to cry on."

"Why not send him a card, Ginger? He can tuck it under his pillow and dream of you every night."

"I'm sure Will likes traditional relationships and sexual fittings, even though Judy had no preference."

"Yeah, I know what you mean, Ginger. Let's talk about Judy and extortion. Who was she mixed up with?"

"Did Alfred Locke discuss the photographs he purchased from Judy? Alfred was so naughty, and he and Judy had the most engaging of sexual encounters. The cost to him was one hundred and fifty thousand dollars. It was worth it to him because his father-in-law founded the bank and his wife would kill him. That's why I wasn't fired. What a shock he didn't mention it to you."

"How did you find out about it?"

"Judy showed me the pictures and the cash. Alfred came crying to me. I told him that he was an idiot - a real moron. He bought the pictures but not the camera, flash-drive, or disc, or whatever she saved them on. You should ask him about it."

"We'll be sure to. Anyone else?"

Ginger sipped her wine and snickered. "Have you interviewed Judy's fellow fantasist, Freddy Nunn - Freddy the Fraud, Sir Freddy the Duplicitous, Fred the Falsifier?"

She snuffed out her cigarette and poured a third glass of wine. "Come on; have one with me; who's going to know?" She stretched her legs, kicked off her heels, and thrust a full chest view in Sweede's direction.

He capped his pen and checked a text message.

She drained her glass. "I'm not defeated by your lack of response, Detective. Where were we?"

"We were discussing Freddy," Sweede reminded her.

"Oh yes, Freddy is, and Judy was, a pathological liar. They engaged in a meeting of the minds, or mindless encounters, two fabricators joined at the hip - or to quote R. A. Salvatore, 'Sane must be boring.' "

CHAPTER THIRTEEN

A bright, blue sign hanging from the door read: "War Room in Use - Keep Out - This Means You." Freddy Nunn stood behind it and stepped back from the full-length mirror. He turned left and right, then forward.

"You're crooked again," Freddy crooned to his nametag. He straightened it and lovingly caressed the title printed above his name, U.S. Park Ranger. Freddy wiped his sweaty brow, placed a trembling hand over his heart, and waited to feel the *thump, thump, thump,* he hoped still beat.

Nunn heaved a sigh of relief and smoothed the wrinkles from his khaki shirt, held high his double chin, stood at attention, and gawked at his reflection. "My God," he thundered, "I've never looked better!"

He waddled to his tripod, set a timer, and positioned himself to the left of a display where he had chalk-marked an X on the floor. He lifted a musket to his chest, cupped its butt with his left hand, and cautiously placed his pudgy right hand on the table.

Freddy breathed deeply and froze. The moment came: three blinding yellow flashes, three clicks, and it was over. He hoped he had not blinked. The photographs of his diorama were more than he had longed for.

The lighting perfectly illuminated each soldier, cannon, horse, ox, wagon, and tree. The strategic planning of the tiny forms had taken him nearly a month, and Freddy wondered how long the American generals had planned their strategy for the fortification of Dorchester Heights.

His replica of the battle included a genuine, white marble model of the Dorchester Heights Monument atop Thomas Park - dedicated to General John Thomas and his troop of brave soldiers. Those British bastards, whatever was left of them, had sailed home across the Atlantic with their tails between their legs. Boston, Massachusetts was free, thanks to Generals Washington and Thomas.

Freddy studied the photographs again. How authoritative and smart he appeared in his uniform. Although a fill-in now, next year he would be a full-time tour guide at Thomas Park, the pinnacle of Dorchester Heights, the pride of South Boston, bigger than the St. Patrick's Day Parade!

Nunn knew his stuff.

He expected to accompany ten or more weekend tourists up ninety-two or so steps to the monument's steeple and, from 130 feet up, point out Boston, Charlestown, Bunker Hill, to Boston Harbor, and Dorchester Bay.

"Of course General Washington knew that Bunker Hill would be one of the main targets, but he and Brigadier General John Thomas outsmarted the British." The tour ended when Freddy guided their binoculars to Quincy Bay and pointed to his own house. They would *ooh* and *ah* and thank him for the tour and their newly acquired knowledge.

Freddy was king of the hill in South Boston - the hill called Thomas Park.

There were no tour guides during the week, and it was nearly 4 P.M. Hungry, Freddy lumbered down to his kitchen and made a peanut butter and jelly sandwich, all the while thinking about what was happening at Thomas Park.

"I better not see any dogs on the hill today; to your owners I say *nay, nay, nay*," he sang. "I hate you poopin' on the grass, and, if I catch you," he laughed, "I'll shoot your furry ass."

Nunn choked on his sandwich, laughed, swallowed, and broke out again in song.

"And to you guys peeing in the bushes and screwing on the grass, I'll bring a gun and shoot your ass!"

Freddy checked his watch in time to check on his neighbors. He tucked a box of cookies under his arm, shoved a can of grape soda into his pocket, and headed to his lookout.

The stairs to the war room creaked under his weight, as he huffed and puffed his way to the top. His telescope and binoculars were perched on tripods. Freddy sat down in front of the binoculars, adjusted their height, and leaned into the lens.

He fine-tuned the focus, then scanned his neighborhood. Maureen Feeney was on vacation, so he ignored her bedroom. Joan Peters was lounging on her deck, sipping wine, and smoking a joint. He mused over a decision to notify the police, decided against it, and focused left.

Clay was packing hamburger into a loaf pan while his wife sat in her wheelchair watching *Judge Jane*. As Freddy adjusted the focus and turned to Thomas Park, a black Crown Victoria traveling up the main drag distracted him, so he zoomed and followed it.

This standard, unmarked police car headed up the causeway and turned right onto Sunrise. Freddy smoothed his uniform, adjusted the tilt of his hat, and dashed down the stairs to stand by the front door.

After the bells chimed once, then twice, he ran his tongue over his lips and flung open the door.

Sweede handed him his card and stepped in.

"Holy shit!" he uttered, as his vision adjusted to the darkness of the foyer and the rotund figure before him.

The brim of Freddy's ranger hat tilted downward and skirted his bushy red brows.

Sweede's gaze moved from the gleaming badge on Freddy's shirt to his dimpled knees that bulged below his khaki shorts. Sturdy double knots secured the laces of his snow white tennis shoes with matching ankle socks.

Ted looked around the room. Piles of newspapers, magazines, and mail lined the walls and covered the tables and chairs. Bags of onions and cartons of chips were stacked on boxes of model ships and planes, the air heavy with the odor of must and decay.

A computer, pristine and new, occupied a desk, half-hidden among soda cans, plastic forks, dirty dishes, and candy wrappers.

Ted and Sweede made their way behind Freddy, who hunkered over the popcorn-speckled rug and sank into a shabby green chair. He crossed his big-boned legs at the ankles, clasped his hands together, and placed them on his lap. The detectives plunked themselves into his dilapidated couch.

Freddy cocked his head. "How can I be of help to you gentleman?"

"You know why we're here?" Sweede began.

"Yes, I do. I can barely talk about it. Excuse me for a moment." He struggled from the chair and tottered from the room.

Ted scratched his head. "Where the hell do you think he's going?"

Sweede yawned. "Where do I think he's going? I think he's going to get laid."

Ted glanced at his watch. "I hope he makes it quick. It's almost 4:30, and I'm having lasagna for dinner!"

"You're having lasagna? Call your wife and tell her to set a plate for me."

Freddy tramped to the parlor, slumped into the chair, and placed a pocket pack of tissues on his lap.

Sweede studied him for a moment. "Everything all right, Freddy?"

"It's been such a terrible year: first my parrot, then Mother, and now Judy. I feel so out of sorts. I don't know if I can go on!" He plucked a tissue from the packet and dabbed at his eyes.

Ted spoke gently. "You're not thinking about harming yourself, are you, Freddy?"

"No, detective, but my heart is broken, just broken in two." He heaved a heavy groan and sobbed into his tissue.

"Judy must have meant a lot to you."

"Well, of course! Judy was such a help to me, especially after Mother's promotion to a higher purpose. She baked macaroni and cheese for me every Thursday night. It was just delicious, just delicious.

"And she planted purple pansies on Mother's grave because I couldn't do it. I just couldn't do it. You know, Judy and I worked together for years. She's the only one who knew I was adopted! She and I have been looking for my birth parents since Mother's passing.

"Judy cares. The letters she writes, I mean wrote, to those agencies for me were so meaningful, so heartfelt. I cried after reading each one," he gulped and grabbed another tissue and mopped the tears that dribbled down his cheeks.

"All those agencies are gone now," he said mournfully. "No need for them I guess. Women's liberation changed that, at least that's what Judy says, or said."

He burst into a fresh outbreak of tears. "I'll never find my true parents now," he bawled. "I'll never know my birthright or take my true place in history."

He plucked another tissue and cleared his nose with an astonishing blow. "We were bosom buddies, kindred spirits really. She would have done anything for me.

"Judy treated me like the son she had but who never grew up. Poor little Jamie - the son - that was *kidnapped and murdered* in infancy!" He shook his head sadly.

"Anyways, our relationship grew to be so much more. But Mr. Goody Two Shoes was so jealous of us. He didn't want her here with me."

Sweede took a deep breath and asked wearily, "Who's Mr. Goody Two Shoes, Freddy?"

"Will, her husband, Mr. Goody Two Shoes, Mr. Do the Right Thing."

"What's wrong with doing the right thing Freddy?"

"Oh, he acted like he was doing the right thing, being helpful and concerned about my wellbeing, but it was just an act. If he hadn't done what she had told him to do, Judy would have let him have it!" he said, punching his fists in the air.

Sweede spoke quietly and deliberately. "Either you're helpful, Freddy, or you're not. So how did he act helpful?"

"Oh, he brought his big macho man saws over here one day and helped me cut down a few saplings out back."

"Anything else he do to be helpful?"

Freddy wiped his brow. "Well, once, when Mother was alive, he repaired the back porch."

Ted broke in. "Not a bad guy to know, Freddy. I wish I had a friend like that."

"He was no friend. It was Judy's doing. She made him do it for me." His voice quivered. "She, she was a love, a real love."

"Freddy, what made her such a love? I mean, what was the attraction other than your spiritual bond and macaroni and cheese?"

Freddy dabbed at the tears in his reddened eyes. "And don't forget those letters she wrote for me!" His voice wavered and cracked.

"Judy was beautiful, inside and out, the most beautiful woman I've ever met - a female Dalai Lama or like Lennon's Yoko - a spiritual guide in a hateful world. Judy was a cross between Yoko and Suzanne Somers!"

"That isn't what we heard," Sweede countered. "We heard she was pretty average looking and that she and her fat butt were a real pain in the ass to Alfred Locke and Ginger Stoolman."

"Who told you that - Ginger? She's nothing but a snooty slut! She was so jealous of the relationship Judy and I shared. Did she try to disgrace my angel's name? Did she?"

"Don't like to break the news to you, Freddy, but Ginger and Judy had their own trip to Nirvana. According to Ginger, things got pretty hot!"

"I don't believe it. That's trash! How dare she say such a thing! Judy would never do such a thing. It would go against our beliefs. We practiced Budslam! We were going to start our own movement - build our own temple!"

Ted wearily closed his note pad and asked the question to which he did not want to hear the answer. "Freddy, what's Budslam?"

Freddy's face brightened. "Well, Detective Ted, Budslam is the combined teachings of Buddha and Islam. Have you ever read the teachings of Buddha, or do you know Islam?" he asked hopefully.

"No, I haven't, and I don't." Ted turned to Sweede. "Ever read the teachings of Buddha or Islam?"

Sweede repositioned his long legs and sat back in amusement. "Nope, I'm still flicking through *SI*'s Swimsuit Issue."

Ted leaned forward. "Freddy, did anything other than truth and beauty ever enter into the relationship, anything of a sexual nature?"

Freddy fumbled with his tissue packet. "What do you mean?"

"Oh come on, Freddy, you know what I mean. You can't be around a woman like that - a real cherub - and not roll around in your feather bed with her!"

Freddy gulped. His tongue shot out and ran across his dry lips.

Ted thumbed through his notebook, found a blank page, and poised his pen. "What about it, Freddy?"

He clasped his hands together, crossed his leg over his knee, and rocked it back and forth, tears pooled in his eyes.

Ted slammed the notebook on the table. Freddy jumped. "I asked you a question Freddy, now what about it? Were you rolling around in the sack with Judy Kennedy?"

He leaned towards Freddy and whispered. "It's so easy to find things out. Forensic investigations are today's way to go. A little DNA leaked on a sheet, a search warrant. Do you watch *CSI* or *Law and Order*?"

Freddy pulled off his ranger hat, blotted the sweat from his drooping curls and forehead, and wiped his eyes. "It was supposed to be so wonderful. Judy was going to divorce Will and marry me as soon as we could afford it."

Ted wrinkled his nose. "How old are you Freddy? Mrs. Kennedy was quite a bit older; were you going to marry an old lady?"

"Age is only numbers! It didn't matter to us because kindred spirits have no age. It's all about experience. Judy winged ahead to make way for my inexperienced spirit. We'll be together in eternity!"

Nunn's face brightened, perhaps stunned by his own comment and newfound enlightenment. He put down his tissues, leaned into the shabby chair, and glanced wistfully at the ceiling. "Judy is planning a place for my soul!"

Ted heaved a sigh. "Freddy, before you put your wings on, tell us when it was that you last saw your angel?"

"I'm not sure. I think it was two weeks ago. No, no, it was three weeks ago, this coming Friday - before she left for Ohio."

"And that's where your angel told you she was flying to, to Ohio?"

"Yes, she was going to Akron, Ohio to settle the estate of her uncle. She said we'd have enough money to be married and to build our temple. Now I'll be going to her funeral instead. I hope Will's happy!" he croaked. "He made her life so miserable. He was so cruel to her."

Sweede narrowed his eyes. "In what way was he cruel?"

"If Judy was here, she'd tell you. I saw that bastard pushing her into their car. They were fighting over a briefcase. Will won. He always wins. He threw it in the trunk, and then he punched Judy in the face, shoved her in the car, and took off!"

Sweede's steely stare locked onto Freddy. "What the hell were you doing when she was getting roughed up? What the fuck were you doing Freddy, sitting on their front stairs eating milk and cookies? You're quite a guy not coming to your babe's rescue!"

Freddy wailed pathetically and dabbed his nose. "Our mantra was that the Force was with us and that no evil would overtake us. I was waiting for it to take over!"

Sweede shot back, "Cut the crap and answer the question. Where the hell were you when he was shoving her around?"

Freddy plucked at the shredded tissue in his hand. "I was counting the number of warbler nests around the pond near their house." He struggled from his seat, ambled into the dining room, and rummaged through a pile of clothes, coat hangers, and old shoe boxes.

He yanked a pair of binoculars from the bottom of the pile and slowly swung them back and forth in front of the exhausted detectives. "I'm a member of the Audubon Society."

Sweede gazed at him thoughtfully. *"You're more than just a member, Freddy, you're a true member - a charter member. You're a fucking bird brain!"*

CHAPTER FOURTEEN

Captain Chung hastily closed the blinds against the torrents of cold rain that pounded the windowpanes of his office, and moped to the cup of hot tea on his desk. He adjusted the bright yellow bowtie nearly hidden below the folds of his neck and slid his copy of the *Daily Racing Form* into the top draw of his desk.

"Who's first? What have we got so far?"

Sweede flipped through his notebook.

"We've got three, maybe four people who have motive to wring Judy Kennedy's neck: Alfred Locke, a bank president she reportedly extorted a hundred and fifty grand from, Ginger, a bisexual or lesbian lover - whatever she is - who dumped her and lost about two hundred grand because of it, a husband who probably wished she had disappeared years ago, and Judy's other lover, Freddy Nunn.

"He's years younger than she was, and she promised to marry him after she inherited her uncle's fortune and dumped her husband. According to Will, Judy didn't have any relatives. Anyway, Nunn says that he saw Judy and Will fighting over a suitcase and that he smacked her around, shoved her in their car, and took off. Alfred Locke, Freddy, Ginger, and Judy all worked together."

Ted adjusted his glasses. "They played together, too. Ginger Stoolman gave us these photos, said that she found a camera hidden in her bedroom. She thinks that Judy must have set it up. Who knows? Look at these."

Chung studied them. "Who are these two?"

Ted leaned over the desk. "That's Judy and the bank president, Alfred Locke; this is Judy and Ginger; and this one is of Freddy and Judy."

Sweede looked over Ted's shoulder and laughed. "What kind of a mortgage rate could I get if I showed these to Alfred Locke? The poor bastard bought the prints but not the Thumb-Drive. He didn't know that these were still floating around!"

Chung cast the photos aside. "So who's lying?"

Ted shrugged. "Maybe everybody."

"What does the husband have to say?"

"We're going over to his house as soon as we leave here."

Chung swallowed the last morsel of his doughnut and wiped his mouth and hands. "Here's the background on both the Kennedys," he said as he passed them a couple of folders. "Interesting facts for you to feed him if he dodges you.

"This may move him to the top of the list for motives. His wife filed three complaints against him in the past year for assault and battery - claimed he tried to strangle her after she found out he was fooling around with a few of the babes that work for him.

"She never followed up or pressed charges. She also claims he has a bunch of illegal Russians working for him. She said that she alerted immigration. I checked with them - they never got a complaint from her.

"I did find out that Will Kennedy hasn't always been the pillar of the community. He's got a rap sheet as long as my arm and I have longer meetings all afternoon."

Chung checked his watch. "So call me as soon as you finish up with him."

CHAPTER FIFTEEN

As the detectives pulled up in front of Kennedy's house, the rain let up and a weak sun broke through the scurrying clouds. Steam rose from Sweede's cup of coffee and clouded the windows, so he cleared a view with the sleeve of his raincoat.

Will's property was neat as a pin, meticulously landscaped, and well maintained – a good investment with a couple of acres of woods around it that sloped towards a pond in the rear.

The detectives knocked and rang the bell but received no answer.

When they walked around the back of the house, Will spotted them from the pond and began the long walk up the steep hill to meet them.

Ted noticed in an alcove a saw nearly hidden behind stacks of drying wood, and moved closer for a better look. A deep, rust colored stain ran along the blade, and bits and pieces of scarlet colored debris clung to its teeth. Ted motioned to Sweede, who did not like the looks of it either.

Will approached and ushered them into the house.

Ted spoke softly. "How are you doing, Will?"

"I'm okay; have a seat."

Ted looked at the reports Chung had given him. "Will, we just want to bring you up to date on the investigation. A few things have come up."

Will shifted in the chair and firmly sat against its cushion - he knew what was coming.

"Your wife made a lot of enemies, Will. She was having affairs and extorting money from her victims."

Will sipped from a bottle of water and carefully placed it on a small side table.

"Did she ever mention Ginger Stoolman, her lover?"

Will blinked. "What do you mean her lover?"

"I mean, that your wife was fooling around with Ginger Stoolman."

Will's thoughts seemed to scatter like dust. A surge of heat flashed through his body, and beads of sweat dotted his forehead.

"I didn't know about Judy and Ginger," he stammered.

Sweede continued. "Did you ever talk with Ginger, meet with her, anything like that?"

"I talked with Ginger a couple of times at bank parties. I didn't know anything about their being lovers." He leaned forward. "Why would Judy tell me anyway? Why would my wife tell me she was having an affair with someone - let alone a female?"

"You tell us. Did she ever talk about ruining Ginger's career, passing around porno of her and her friends at the bank after Ginger dumped her?"

He chucked the photos on Will's lap. "Did she ever show you these?"

Kennedy glanced at the top photo and handed them to Sweede. "No," he whispered.

"How about Alfred Locke, your racquetball buddy? Did you and your wife share the loot she extorted from him? She was screwing him too!" Sweede waved the photos in Will's face. "These pictures are pretty hot! Maybe you two sat by the fire on cold nights, getting your own jollies and counting the money!"

"No!"

Ted bowed his head and thoughtfully folded his hands. "How about Freddy? He said that you smacked your wife around over a suitcase full of money!"

"No, I didn't. I didn't do that."

The room seemed to tilt and whirl around him. To stop the dizziness, he needed a focal point and stared at his shoes.

Ted pressed. "Were you and your wife in Ohio a couple of weeks ago? We heard her uncle died, and she was out there collecting her inheritance. Is that where the suitcase full of money came from?"

"No. I told you, she didn't have any relatives, there was no suitcase full of money, and we weren't in Ohio, check with the airlines."

"Freddy said you were there, maybe you drove."

Will glared at Ted. "The hell with Freddy! What does he know?"

Ted searched Will's face. "Take it easy. I'm only the messenger. We can't dismiss Freddy. After all, he was sleeping with your wife. She must have whispered something about Ohio and the money in his ear while they were rolling around in the sack."

Kennedy's voice cracked. "I don't believe it."

"Will, it's true," Ted nodded sadly.

He turned to his partner. "What have you got, Sweede?"

"The DNA samples from the hairbrush, sea strainer, and the hand that was caught in the lobster netting all match. A little kid found your wife's hand, Will. She threw up when she saw it. The kid's in counseling."

Will looked at his clenched hands. "I'm sorry to hear that."

"The hand was severed at the wrist bone - cut so clean a surgeon could have done it. Freddy said you have quite a collection of saws. Like the one out back.

"You and your cleaning crew ever do body clean-ups? Do you clean up over at Harvard Medical School? Maybe you picked up a really good saw over there; you know the type that surgeons use, something that cuts really clean.

"Someone chopped your wife up and dumped her in Quincy Bay, and my bet is on you. Do you have a boat, Will?"

"I have a kayak and a skiff."

"Any chance we could take a look at them?"

Will thought for a moment and took a deep breath. His muscles relaxed, and he sat back in the chair, his eyes gleaming.

"No!"

"Why not? Didn't you wash the blood off yet? Too busy fooling around with your help? We know all about it. Judy filed an assault and battery charge against you. Everyone at the bank saw the marks on her neck. You tried to strangle her."

Will raised his eyebrows and leisurely shook his head no.

Sweede caught a trace of amusement on Kennedy's face.

"Yes, you did. She caught you fooling around, and you tried to shut her up. Didn't want your Russian babes shipped back to the fucking Kremlin! Judy was going to turn you in to the Feds. She was all set to ruin you and your business.

"You finally shut her up for good. Everyone knows about your marriage, Will. It was a big sham. Your wife out doing her thing, you home mowing the lawn and doing the wash, afraid to stand up to her.

"But you finally snapped! Shut her up for good. You cut her up with your saw and dumped her in the bay! That's what happened, Will.

"You knew about Ginger and Freddy, and you knew about Alfred. Maybe they paid you off to do their dirty work. Were you in collusion with them? Did you tell them you were a wife chopper?

"Did Ginger hire a bigger boat so you could fit all of Judy's body parts in it? She asked us to send her condolences to you, thought you may want to cry on her shoulder. You're not the guy we thought you were. You're not any AJ squared away.

"You're not the nice guy that everyone thinks you are. You're a fake. Your wife was a fake too, but you're the one with the rap sheet. Rap sheets show patterns in behavior. Maybe you and Judy had fun with Ginger, and she liked you more than she did your wife. Maybe both of you wanted her out of the way!"

Ted interrupted Sweede's rant. "Knock it off, Sweede. The guy just lost his wife. Even if he did kill her, it must have been temporary insanity. Look at him, he's in shock. He can barely get a word out! Everyone knows Judy was crazy.

"Imagine what he's been through all these years. He just snapped. Who wouldn't understand that after all he's been through?"

Ted pulled his chair up closer to Kennedy. "There are plenty of guys like you out there, Will. And, average guys like you and me on a jury understand what it's like: the accusations, sarcasm, the screaming, and hollering. Will, you've been emotionally abused!"

Sweede scoffed at Ted. "Plenty of guys put up with shit like that, but they don't kill their wives!" He turned to Will and glared.

"When was the last time she let you poke her? Last year? Five years ago? Ten years ago, on your birthday? Did you have to wine and dine her, buy her jewelry just to get a little feel? You're better off if you just let it all out, get it off your chest," he bellowed.

Sweede pointed his finger at Will. "It was premeditated. Freddy Nunn already gave his statement. Ginger Stoolman and Alfred Locke are on the way to the station right now. They're ready to spill their guts. They may have helped you, but you're the wife chopper! You murdered your wife!"

Kennedy leveled his glare at Sweede. "Prove it."

CHAPTER SIXTEEN

Ginger had carefully screwed the cap onto her bottle of scarlet polish and blew on her wet nails when the intrusive buzzing of the intercom sounded.

"Oh, shit!"

With her index finger and thumb, she warily lifted the receiver. "I'm busy, Dot. What do you want?"

She listened for a moment, slammed the receiver, and marched to Alfred's office. "What the hell does he want that's so damn important at ten in the morning? It better not be anything about Judy extorting money from him," she grumbled, "or I'll have a show-and-tell meeting with his bride."

She stomped into his outer office and stopped at Dot's desk. "What does he want with me?" she snapped.

Dot sheepishly looked from her ledger. "I'm sorry, Ms. Stoolman, I don't know. We've had such a busy morning, and it's not even ten."

"Why is his door closed?"

Dot closed the ledger and anxiously straightened papers in front of her. "He's meeting with Freddy Nunn, but it wasn't scheduled. I'm sure he'll be right out."

"What do you mean 'not scheduled'? You must know what it's about!"

"Ms. Stoolman, I don't, I really don't know what it's about, but Mr. Locke is expecting you, so I'm sure Freddy will be right out."

"Well, get me a black coffee while I'm waiting. And make sure it's fresh!"

"Yes, of course, Ms. Stoolman." Dot excused herself and hastily headed for the break room.

Ginger checked her nails and leaned against the wall, tapping the toe of her shoe on the floor while eyeing Alfred's door. Freddy emerged from the office - pale and drawn. He eyed Ginger, squared his shoulders, threw his head back, and streamed by her.

Dot watched as Ginger stormed past Alfred, who quietly closed the door behind her.

"This is a first," she whispered into the phone. "Ginger is in there crying. I can hear Alfred blasting her. Oh, I've got to go, they're coming out," she said and hastily hung up.

Ginger emerged haughty and infuriated, artfully adjusting with a forefinger her red-framed glasses. Alfred dragged behind her.

She abruptly stopped, spun around, and glared at him. "I'm calling it a day. I've got an upset stomach - some people make me sick!"

•••

The bar at Gemelli's was packed by noon, but Ginger found an empty stool and bellied up. Jimmy Gemelli hustled to her. "Need a menu, Ginger?"

"No, give me the usual, but straight up with a twist."

He set her up. "You look like you just lost your best friend."

"It's not my friend. It's my boss, and he's hardly my best friend - he's a moron! I think he's trying to pull a fast one on me. I hope he drowns in his swimming pool!"

"You know what they say, Ginger," said Jimmy, slicing up a lemon. "Don't get mad, get even."

"You bet your ass I will!" She sat sipping her drink.

"Jimmy, change the channel to seven." The footage showed the Feds escorting a couple of shackled financial advisors to a waiting car. The crawl read that the two had embezzled nearly eleven million dollars from their elderly clients - somewhere out on the West Coast.

Ginger pondered her own problems. *The bank examiners would be in first thing in the morning and it would not take them long to figure out that Judy had not embezzled all that money without help. Alfred Locke was such a liar and a fake. He better come up with something and fast. That dope, Freddy, was afraid of his own farts.*

She looked at the television and murmured; "You guys were stupid. What happened to you is not going to happen to me."

Jimmy's voice interrupted her thoughts. "Another one, Ginger?"

She nodded, and he rapidly wiped the counter and delivered her drink.

"Hey, Ginger, did they ever charge anyone with Judy's murder? I haven't heard much about it. You two used to come in a lot. You must miss her."

"Jimmy, have you been living in a cave? They're probably going to charge her husband. And frankly, I don't give two shits about what happened to her; I don't miss her, and neither does anyone else, except for that Baby Hughie of a big shit head."

Jimmy leaned against the bar and chuckled. "Oh, I know; you don't have to tell me. You mean Freddy, the one that wore his park ranger getup in here on the Fourth of July and ordered an extra-large Shirley Temple with six cherries and a large order of fries."

"You got it," she spat. "Cash me out Jimmy; I've got to get home and make a few calls."

●●●

Ginger fumbled with the key, flung open the door, threw her briefcase on the couch, and punched in numbers on her cell. "Let me speak with Barry. What? Are you new to the firm? Of course I'm a client. He's been handling my legal affairs for over ten years. Just tell him who it is!"

Barry picked up immediately. "What's up Ginger?"

"Barry, a few issues have come up at the bank that could implicate me in a messy situation. The examiners will be in first thing in the morning. I need a plan. I need to see you tonight."

"Ginger, I can't see you until Monday. I've got to be in New York by six tonight."

"Oh, Barry, it'll only take an hour. I'm telling you, I need a plan."

"I can't do it," he said firmly. "Come in on Monday at nine, and we'll talk."

CHAPTER SEVENTEEN

Ginger sat on her terrace, swathed in a heavy, black wool sweater. Sensing dampness and a raw chill, she drew the sweater closer to her chest.

The settling dusk carried cool whiffs of a coming rain. Beyond her parking lot, a thick woods rose dark and silent, its treetops smudged in a descending fog. Disturbed by the stillness, she swirled the cubes in her glass around and around and listened to their chinking and tinkling.

A sharp ring of the phone interrupted. "What? Are you sure? When did Judy give it to you? So you're saying that she double crossed me, and you have a quarter of a million. Why tell me? Why not keep it yourself?" Ginger gnawed on her nail and thought over his reply.

"Now you listen to me you moron," she hissed. "I wouldn't be having a conversation with you, if this didn't make sense. False accounts were her idea, not mine, and you went along with it.

"I'll be there in half an hour and meet you out back of your house. And get this, bud, don't try to jerk me around again or I'll blow your brains out. I don't care who you are! They'll be picking you up with a fork and knife - understand?"

She packed her .38, secured its shoulder strap, slid in to her firing jacket, fastened its polished metal buttons, and left.

•••

The wind picked up and blew across the cold, black water below her. Ginger trembled at the squawk of a lone duck calling through the fog and damp night air, drew her knees to her chest, and wrapped her arms around them.

An opossum, tiny babies clutched to their mother's back, scampered across the yard.

Ginger hastily brushed a stray tear from her cheek, slid a shiny metal flask from her pocket, took a good belt of vodka, hitched her body back a bit, and pressed it against the rough bark of the rustling elm that loomed above her.

She studied the house. From her outlook, she could see the walkway leading to the front stairs, and the back of the house lay in full view.

There was no sign of him.

The polished silver buttons on her jacket reflected the lone light coming from the porch. She swore softly, "I should have worn another jacket."

He sat hidden among the thorny branches and soft leaves of the thick bushes, studying her form through night-vision glasses and aimed the barrel of his gun at her head.

How bizarre her platinum hair looked on such a black night, nearly iridescent green in the light's reflection. It blew stiff and dry like the tufted marsh grasses of winter that blow back and forth but never bend in the icy winds.

It offended him, so he lowered his aim, to hit her between the eyes. Then, as soft a sound as the swooshing leaves around her, she heard his voice, "Got you, Ginger."

She jerked her head around, but it was too late. One shot, faintly heard, and Ginger Stoolman lay still forever.

He gingerly removed the keys from her jacket, dragged her body from a shallow depression, past overgrown lilac bushes and across damp grass, and dumped it into the trunk of her car. He shoved the guns under the seat, slowly drove along winding curves to a granite quarry and slid into neutral the gleaming red, three thousand pound Porsche.

Once stationed against the bumper, he dug in his heels, groaned, and shoved with all his might; the Porsche slid over the sill. It screeched and scraped against the granite walls, ricocheted off a ledge, flipped, and spiraled like a rocket into hell.

"Holy Shit!" he screamed over the stupendous splash, and fell against a tree gasping and sweating. A searing heat swelled in his stomach and seared to his throat.

Ginger's killer bent over and puked, coughing and spitting his way to the main road and past the darkened store fronts and flickering streetlights. Abruptly, he stopped.

There it was again and again - raindrops! A chilling thought gripped him; *I don't want to catch cold,* so he picked up his pace and jogged home.

•••

The youthful face of Kyle Cameron came on camera. "Now don't go reaching for the umbrellas folks. Just a few overnight sprinkles passing by - a fast moving front coming down from the Great Lakes and Chicago to Boston and out to sea by the time you wake up!"

Anchor Caitlin Keene chided him. "Oh, Kyle, what if the folks out there need to be up as early as our morning team? Three in the morning comes pretty early."

Kyle chuckled and pointed. "I promise you and our viewers that we'll be all clear by then. Tomorrow promises to be a number ten day with high's in the low to mid-seventies, plenty of sun, and no wind. Sorry, you sailors. Hey, folks why not join me and the night team for our annual blood drive at the …"

He clicked off the weather, showered, then crawled into bed and waited for a peaceful sleep that never came. Vague visions emerged and leisurely meshed into murky shapes and hues that melted into a multitude of dreamy delusions, auras, and uninvited apparitions.

"Time's up," shouted Judy. She pointed the bright purple barrel of a cannon to a map behind a colorful spinning wheel. "I'm an oceanographer. Well, not really, but I am an ocean traveler. The correct answer is the Atlantic Ocean. The Gulf Stream flows from the southwest to northeast toward the British Isles and passes the southernmost point of Stellwagen Bank." She shook out the cannon barrel and wrapped it around her shoulders.

"Hey, Judy," he yelled, "is that what you call magic? How did you do that?"

"I'm no magician!" She pulled out a pistol hidden under her jacket and fired at him. *Bang!*

He examined the hole in his leg and wondered if a paper punch had made it. "Hey, there's no blood, and I can see clear through. Does this mean I can spin the wheel again?"

"No, it doesn't. You said Pacific, and that's that," snapped Ginger.

He stomped his foot. "It is the Pacific. And it costs a lot of money; I've got pictures to prove it!"

"Who cares, I just want to sing."

Freddy nodded to her. "Go on Ginger, sing your heart out."

Alex Freebeck snatched the microphone from Ginger and winked at Judy. "Now sing, sing along with me, girls! Sing loud and proud! Let's sing the row boat song! Row, row, row…"

"Stop it, Alex," commanded Sweede. "The buzzer says your time is up!"

Ted nodded his head. "That's right."

"I'm not finished."

Will spoke up. "Alex, you're more than finished. The buzzer stays on until you sit down."

"This is incredible!" said Alex. He tucked the microphone into the front of his shorts. "And by the way," he said, pointing at them, "I'm telling my mother!"

Ginger rolled her eyes. "You don't scare me, you moron! Canadians don't have mothers. They have 'coon skin caps, platinum hair, and hockey pucks. The buzzer stays on!"

"You're not the only one who controls the buzzer," cried Alex.

Will and Freddy fought over the microphone. Will won, shot Alex, and then took aim at the buzzer.

Freddy stood looking down at Alex. "Is your real name Alfred, like, Alfred Hitchcock or like Alfred E. Newman? Because if it is, then Ginger's right, the buzzer stays on!"

He awoke trembling and mumbling. "It was only a dream, but that buzzing." Groping his alarm clock, he grumbled, "It's over," and fell back to sleep.

CHAPTER EIGHTEEN

Ronan anxiously circled his pen and barked. Marybeth hastily slid into her robe and watched him from the bathroom window, as he barked and howled.

"Oh, I hope he doesn't wake the neighbors," she murmured, hurrying to the back hall to flick on the lights. Ronan stood quivering, watching the back door. Marybeth cautiously looked for skunks, saw none, and hurried to his pen. "What is it, Ronan?"

His eyes glistened in the darkness, and he barked again.

Marybeth looked around helplessly. "Come in, come into the house. Come on, Ronan, Gillan is on his way home. No barking. You'll wake up the whole neighborhood!"

Streaming head lights finally appeared in driveway. "I'm so glad you're home! Ronan's been barking off and on for the past hour, and he won't come in."

Gillan grabbed a leash from the back seat. "I'll take him for a walk."

"Honey, it's nearly eleven. Do you think you should?"

"I'll be right back."

He and his dog hustled through dark, quiet streets and marsh. Gillan flipped on his flashlight. Ronan pulled ahead to the shoreline and stopped at the foot of a steep incline of granite boulders, shuddering and yanking on his leash.

Gillan shook his head. "We'll come back in the morning."

He marked the spot with a few rocks and headed home. Ronan settled in his pen and slept; Gillan lay awake waiting for sunrise.

Dawn broke to an overcast sky and blustery winds, but neither dampened Marybeth's spirit. Gillan was on vacation for two weeks, their bags were packed, and, in a few days, they would be relaxing in Bar Harbor, Maine.

A spicy aroma of sizzling bacon drifted throughout the house. Gillan leaned comfortably against the kitchen counter, sipping coffee and looking out a spacious window to the backyard.

Marybeth moved around him, humming to the soft morning music on the radio. She took a few eggs from the fridge, stopped, and kissed him on the cheek. "Fried or scrambled?"

"Any English muffins?"

"Yes, Honey."

"Then I'll have scrambled."

Marybeth turned the sizzling bacon and broke the eggs into a bowl. "What are you looking at Gillan?" she asked, slipping her arm around his waist.

"My gosh, they didn't predict high winds! Look at the Pittsley's flag. It's blowing straight out!" she exclaimed while peering at the swaying trees.

She briskly patted his butt. "You're still as tight as a drum. Maybe you should bring in the lawn furniture."

"I'm going to take Ronan out first to where we went last night."

"Is he still pacing?"

"Yeah, he won't stay in his shelter. Look at him, still whining and watching the door, waiting for me. He knows something's up."

Marybeth sighed. "Gillan, maybe the sound of the wind scares him, or maybe he just wants to come in."

"Hold off on the eggs."

He checked his gear pack for water, gloves, pencil, and paper, grabbed his black slicker, and headed out the door.

Through the rain-spattered window, she watched Ronan, dancing and prancing in mind-whirling circles as Gillan approached.

He crouched, clipped a thick brown leather leash to Ronan's collar, and vigorously rubbed his fingers into the deep, rust-colored fur on the panting shepherd's neck.

"We've got work to do. And you know what that means. When we're done, you're going to get what you love most," he said, swinging a bright blue tug toy before Ronan's watchful eyes. The shepherd yelped once.

"Let's go, buddy, it's time to move."

Marybeth watched them hustle up the street. She thought how alike she was to Ronan, jubilant and wagging her own tail whenever Gillan came within fifty feet of her.

She adored his looks, the sky blue eyes and glistening white hair that set him apart from everybody else. She believed it was God's way of telling the world that he walked the planet to do unique work, as distinctive as his looks. Anyone could spot Gillan Murphy from a mile away.

She moved a magnet on the fridge and took down her photo of him and Ronan. "You love that dog, probably more than you love me, but that's all right. You two have important work to do."

When he decided on a Belgian Malinois, Marybeth had been wary but was impressed with the dog's intensity and intelligence. She studied the photo for a long time. "Ronan is just like you, Gillan, intense and intelligent."

•••

Perfectly bred in Ireland and imported to the States, Ronan had been trained to recognize the scent of gunpowder and the sixty or so additives that the bad guys use to build or conceal the scent of bombs and weapons of destruction. The dog's training never ended because new elements or compounds were always being added.

Gillan named the shepherd, Ronan, after the Irish saint who had protected the people of his own village, which is what Lieutenant Gillan Murphy and Ronan did together: protect the public. They traveled over the state for Homeland Security and sometimes the FBI, pinpointing bombs planted in church confessionals, school cafeterias, and shopping malls.

They located stashes of munitions - guns and assault weapons in drug dens, drop-in centers, school lockers and libraries, cozy cottages and cathedrals, and SUVs packed with picnic baskets, beach chairs, beach balls, and babies. Ronan tracked the scent of gunpowder, sometimes over a quarter of a mile away and right to its source, if the wind were right.

Ronan never missed his mark.

When not with Ronan, Gillan was with his team of scuba divers. He was a master diver and a patient, exacting instructor schooling them in the art of operating marine sonar equipment, rescuing boaters, or searching for bodies in the state's lakes, ponds, and coastal waters.

Gillan's job was so emotionally demanding that Marybeth tried to make their home, his haven.

•••

Marybeth moved to the window and watched as the morning light gave way to an eerie gray sky; billowing black clouds loomed in the distance. She zipped-up her sweatshirt to the sound of the screaming wind.

Torrents of rain battered the windows and distorted her garden into streams of blues, pinks, and purples wildly swaying in the savage squalls. Brutal blasts of wind tore through the trees, ripping leaves and splitting branches from the great swaying forms that lent such peace and shade to the backyard in the sizzling, summer heat.

She wondered how many outdoor barbeques she and Gillan had prepared over the past years for Sweede, Ted, Mars Starr, J. D., and the rest of the detectives, drinking beer, grilling steaks, and trading stories about cadaver and bomb finds, drug busts, bank robberies, murder and debating whether German or English should be used for dog commands. Marybeth moved away from the windows.

What was taking him so long?

With a blast of wind, the door blew open, and Gillan and Ronan dashed into the safety of the cozy kitchen.

"Oh no, you two are soaked. Stay where you are!" She quickly returned with a stack of towels and wiped Ronan's ears. "What's going on, Gillan?"

"I'm not sure," he said, vigorously drying his head and face. "Ronan's still on to it. We tried to go back to where we were last night, but the wind gusts must be up to seventy-five miles per hour.

"Haskins said it's a microburst and could be over in an hour. The sun is shining southwest and to where we were headed, but, from our street and up, it's blowing like a Nor'easter. I brought the lawn chairs in. Did you watch the weather?"

"I couldn't find the clicker."

"Here, take the towel. I've got to make a few calls."

"Wait a minute, Gillan. How far did you get?"

He shook his head in exasperation. "Marybeth, I got as far as Haskins' house."

"Who's Haskins?"

"He's the writer who bought the big gray house on the end of the street last year."

"Do you mean that guy who wears those Hawaiian shirts and smokes cigars?"

"Yeah, that's who I mean. He was out there in his yard and let us cut through, but the wind really picked up. We couldn't go any farther, but Ronan is raring to go. I'll check it out as soon as the wind dies down."

"Oh, Gillan, what about our vacation?"

"It won't take long. If it's a microburst, we're in luck. They don't cover much ground, maybe a mile or two. They're fierce - hit and runs'- and then it's over! Ronan wants to search. If there's something there, he'll find it."

Marybeth contemplated their vacation plans. "Gillan, you know, if Ronan smelled gunpowder last night, maybe it was just kids with fireworks or the Tappers shooting at those turkeys again. They live south of here. I drove by their house yesterday. The turkeys were sitting on the garage roof! And Mrs. Tapper was out there taking pictures of them!"

"Nice try, Marybeth. We'll get to Bar Harbor eventually."

CHAPTER NINETEEN

Alfred eyed the clock on the wall and continued pacing the length of his office. He checked his watch again and buzzed the intercom.

"Dot, call me as soon as Ms. Stoolman arrives. It's almost eight, and she was due in at seven-thirty. In fact, call her right now and get back to me. The examiners are due in at nine. She needs to be here right now!"

Pain killers shook in his trembling hand, and he fumbled them into his mouth before washing them down with coffee. Alfred swabbed the sweat from his face and dropped into his chair.

"I have to stay positive, I need to look ahead," he gasped. "I can't stop now. I have more than my share, and in three weeks, I'll be out of here. They'll never find me."

Reflection gripped him. *He had never seen Ginger so unglued, she thought she was smarter than everyone else - smarter than Judy anyway - and everybody was smarter than Freddy, that stupid little dink! They had all played the game, and he, Alfred Locke, had outsmarted them. Well, show time!*

He straightened his tie, checked his teeth in the mirror, and barreled to the reception area. "How did you make out, Dot? Did you get hold of her?"

"I'm so sorry, Mr. Locke, she's not picking up."

"Hmm…well, I better go check on her. Give me her address."

Dot looked at him quizzically. "You don't normally do such things, Mr. Locke, but, here it is. Why not send Freddy? He'll be in any minute. That way, you can still get your swimming laps in."

Locke looked aside from her. "No swimming for me today, Dot. I'm too busy. I need to find Ginger! And Freddy has plenty to do this morning."

"Well, stay dry and batten down the hatches," she squealed. "It's raining cats and dogs!"

•••

Bracing himself against his white Corolla, Alfred pulled his collar up and hat down against the raging storm and slogged his way through the puddles and rivulets of water that seeped into his tasseled loafers. "No one said a damn thing about a storm!" he grumbled.

Ginger's condo lay ahead; he trudged through her parking lot and past a sleek array of BMWs, Audis, and Porches still parked there. "How the hell does anyone afford one of these, if the damn parking lot is so damn full of them at this time of day? Does anyone work around here?"

A blast of wind snatched his hat and propelled it across the parking lot and under a Lexus. Even so, Alfred Locke plodded on.

The lobby's camera focused on him, and a ceiling vent propelled a steady stream of chilly air to his dripping head. He shook off the water, rang her buzzer, and waited.

When Ginger did not answer, Alfred rang again and stood studying the sopping cuffs of his slacks. "*Achoo, achoo, achoo,*" he blasted in quick succession.

"Oh Jesus, Mary, and Joseph, please don't let me catch a cold." He hastily pressed the buzzer for a third time and checked his watch. "Here's a few more for you, Ginger," he sneered, "Morse code style!" and buzzed repeatedly, in brief, broken, bleeps.

"The hell with this!" he muttered and frantically fumbled for his phone. "Dot, call Ginger's brother and find out if she's contacted him."

"Oh, I did. I did, Mr. Locke. I got him out of bed. There's a time difference you know. He hasn't heard from her. I checked her office again, the door was still locked, so we opened it. She's not there. And the bank examiners are due in at any minute."

"All right Dot, "I'll be right in."

•••

Solemn-faced bank examiners filed into the cool blues and grays that decorated the conference room in a pseudo sense of security and no-nonsense conversations that the trustees favored. The clicking sound of safety locks echoed above the shuffling of documents and whispered conversations. Calculators sat at lengthy intervals on the highly polished conference table.

Dot wheeled into the hushed room a cart laden with pastry, bagels, and coffee and stationed it left of the water cooler. She fluttered around, straightening blinds and paper cups. Her pencil-thin brows furrowed at the sight of a stray paper clip under a chair, and she swooped down, plucked it up, gave a tight little smile to the group around her, and flew from the room.

Alfred Locke sauntered passed her in the hall and took his place at the head of the great table, wringing his hands and clearing his throat. The bank examiners looked at him. His beige suit hung wrinkled and damp from his pear-shaped frame, and his face appeared pale and drawn.

He smiled dimly and introduced himself. "Our key staff is available to meet at your convenience. The blue folders that you received earlier contain lists of departments, contacts, and any relevant information that you may need. Our Junior VP, Ms. Stoolman, has been delayed.

"Contact my secretary, Dot, - Dorothy Mott - at extension 3846 for anything that you may need. I'm at extension 3920." He wandered from the room and rambled up to Dot's desk. "Has she arrived yet?"

She tightened her lips. "No, she hasn't, Mr. Locke."

"And you've tried her phone again?"

A shadow of deep concern crossed her face, but Dot spoke with purpose and determination. "She's not picking up, Mr. Locke, but I'll keep trying!"

"Yes, yes, keep trying, Dot," he croaked, before heading for his office.

Between sips of hot tea, Dot took a small bite from her raspberry Danish. "Ginger Stoolman, that bitchy slut, is going to catch bloody hell when she shows up," she murmured. "Life can be so good when Ginger isn't." She meticulously wiped her desktop of any stray crumbs and returned to work.

Alfred sat breathless and shaking. A gnawing pain in his stomach had worsened. He gulped some antacid, burped, headed for the toilet, and emerged later with a new resolve. "Dot, call Detective Swenson. Here's his card. Tell him it's an emergency and ask him to come by as soon as possible."

She studied the dark circles under his eyes. "Of course, of course, I will. And excuse me for saying this, Mr. Locke, but you should get your exercise in. That's what the doctor ordered. Why not do a few laps at the pool? It won't take long, and it's going to be a stressful few weeks with the bank examiners in."

Alfred wiped his hand over his mouth and chin. "I know, I know. Call my wife and ask her to bring my swim trunks and nose clip in. They're in the back seat of her car. She stayed at her mother's last night; she can drop them off on her way home.

"And, Dot, when the detectives arrive, notify me at once!"

CHAPTER TWENTY

S weede and Ted pulled into the parking lot and stopped with a splash. They hunkered in their raincoats and ran against the headwinds to the safety of the bank. Dot sprang from her chair and quickly ushered them to Locke's office.

Ted shook the water from his coat. "I can't remember the last time it rained like this! My wife said that the sun's shining on our street."

Alfred stood quietly trembling.

Sweede watched as the banker vaguely felt for the leather chair behind himself and sank into the safety of its gray cushions. His normally flushed faced appeared white, eerie, and trance-like.

"Things not going well today, Alfred? I know you said the bank examiners were coming in, and your secretary said that Ginger Stoolman hasn't showed up. What's going on?"

Alfred pulled a white hankie from his pocket and wiped his face. His voice cracking, Locke stammered and spoke in whispered words of desperation - like a man pleading for his life at gun-point. "We've been trying to reach her all morning. She's missing and I, well, please understand me. I could be implicated, if she's not found. It's just a misunderstanding on Ms. Stoolman's part."

Alfred shook his great bald head. "Perhaps I spoke in haste. Perhaps I've been naïve about Will Kennedy. Have you arrested him yet?" He dabbed and mopped the sweat from his face. "I have something here that could possibly implicate him in the…"

He brought his trembling hand to his mouth and burped. "Excuse me."

Sweede shot a quizzical glance at Ted, so they turned their attention to the squirming figure before them.

"What is it that you're not telling us?"

Alfred clutched his head. A low, pitiful moan escaped as he struggled from the chair and moved unsteadily across the room in short, measured steps. He neared the water cooler, fumbled for a cup, swayed forward, wobbled backward, grabbed his chest, and collapsed.

CHAPTER TWENTY ONE

Rose sat squeezed in a wheelchair with her arms folded over her chest glaring at her daughters. They were pouring over hundreds of multicolored swatches of fabric for drapes; the decorator needed a decision by the end of the day. Rose would be moving into Marsh House the first of next month, that is, if she didn't change her mind *again*. Christine handed her a sample of material. "Mom, what do you think of this print?"

Rose wrinkled her nose and threw it on the table. "Christine, if I've told you once, I've told you a million times that I don't like small prints. They're too busy. I want something big and bold, something bright and happy - like I am!"

Natalie rolled her eyes and flipped through another book of swatches. "Ma, the living room at Marsh House is smaller than this living room. A big, splashy, print won't work in your new apartment."

"Yes, it will!"

"Have it your way Ma," she said handing her another swatch. "The flowers are soft pink and bigger than basketballs."

Rose inspected the material, "I'll take it, but only if you can get it in a brighter pink, a hot pink, like the color of my lipstick!"

Natalie groaned. She cautiously turned her head to the left and then to the right and tried to massage the spasm that gripped the back of her neck. "Okay, Ma, I'll call Mrs. Gaynor and let her know."

She spoke with the decorator, turned the kettle on for tea, and placed three cups and saucers on a tray. "I bought some cold cuts," she shouted from the kitchen. "Anyone want a sandwich?"

Rose hollered back. "Bring me some macaroons, but only if they're still soft!"

Christine put the swatches aside. "Mom, I just bought them. They're fresh."

Rose tapped her fingers on the table. "You can never tell. And why do you keep eyeing that piece of material?"

"Mom, what ever happened to that afghan you knitted? It had three different shades of pink in it. It would match the material you picked out. You could use it as a lap blanket in the winter."

Rose waved Christine off. "Oh, that. I forgot about that lap blanket. It must be in the cedar chest with the rest of the afghans that no one wants, and the sweaters that I've knitted for you and your sister that neither of you will wear. They've been up there for years."

Natalie's voice rose in frustration. "That's because the sweaters and afghans you knit are gaudy looking!" She cleared the swatches from the table, sauntered into the kitchen, returned with a plate of macaroons which she slid on the table. "Personally I wouldn't wear a sweater or put a blanket on my lap that's the color of a tangerine, an over-ripe lemon or the inside of a watermelon. And neither would Christine. Why don't you knit something in a color that suits us, colors that you see us wearing? Why does it always have to be the colors that you like?"

"The colors that I like are happy colors! I wish I had daughters like me, happy people who like happy colors!"

Natalie gasped in amazement. "Happy! You've never been happy or positive about anything. It's always the same with you - the tea is too hot and the ice cream is too cold."

Christine hastily put a sandwich together. "Natalie, Mom, please!"

Rose glared at Natalie and ignored Christine's stare.

"Mom, the point is you've made a decision about the material for the drapes, which brings up another point; we need to think about what to do with things like the sweaters and afghans and anything else you've collected or saved over the years that you don't want. We need to start cleaning out the attic and sorting things out. We'll start in the cedar chest."

They finished their lunch in silence. Rose looked up at the clock and tinkered with the brake release on the wheel chair then pushed off toward the living room. "I'm going in to watch my stories."

Natalie watched Christine head up stairs. "Where are you going?"

"I'm going up to the sewing room; I need to open the cedar chest and look for that afghan."

"I'll come too."

Christine had always thought that the sewing room was the coziest room in the house. Her childhood memories were filled with images of her mother hunched over the sew-ing machine in that sunny place making or mending clothes for her children, a yellow tape measure and red pins' cushion a hands reach away. The sewing room wasn't a room so to speak, it was a beautifully windowed alcove centered between the four bedrooms.

The handsome cedar chest had been crafted by Rose's grandfather back in the old country and shipped to the States along with his daughter Ann and her groom around the turn of the century. Rose was born years later and often recalled helping her mother fold woolen blankets and clothes and snugly storing them in there for the summer.

Christine remembered playing in the sewing room as a child and walking her dolls along the rich, amber, grain pat-terns of the cedar chest. It still stood - magnificent in its ancient and ornate beauty against the rear wall of the sewing room, away from the windows and out of the sun's damaging rays.

Natalie knelt on the floor beside her sister and opened the old chest. She pulled out a couple of bright, orange sweaters - frowning, she placed them aside.

"Look Natalie, here's Phillip's high school football sweater and your cheering sweater!"

"Oh, let me have that!" She smiled and held it up to her chest. "I didn't know that Ma kept this. I wonder if there's anything else of mine in here." Natalie rummaged down and felt a shoebox. She slid the ribbon off and opened it. "Look Christine, letters from Dad to Ma, he wrote them from Korea during the war."

Christine packed them back up in the shoe box. "They're private; we'll have to bring them down to her."

Natalie dug further. "And here's another one," she said waving it around. She stopped and read the envelope. Her eyes clouded over. "Christine, this one is addressed to you."

"To me? There's no return address, and it's been opened. I can't read the post mark date, but it was mailed in Boston."

Natalie sighed. "Just open it!"

Christine slipped the letter out but abruptly paused. "Is that Mom calling?"

Natalie listened for a moment. "Yes, it is!" She scrambled to her feet and raced down the stairs. "Christine, call an ambulance! Ma says she having a heart attack!"

CHAPTER TWENTY TWO

C aptain Chung finished his toast and hastily brushed the crumbs from the front of his pink shirt and ample lap. "I just got off the phone with the DA's office. They've got enough evidence to charge Will Kennedy for the murder of his wife."

"Did we miss something?" Sweede asked sarcastically.

"Oh, that's right. I didn't tell you the plan; the DA didn't call me until late last night. I sent Gillan and his divers over to the pond in back of Kennedy's house this morning. They found his wife's cell and pocketbook there on the bottom."

Chung glanced at Sweede who sat nearby with his arms crossed over his chest before continuing. "Mars Starr brought his cadaver-sniffing dog, Tonto, up to Kennedy's place. The only scent of blood and rotting tissue that the dog tracked was around the area where the saw was. And there wasn't another trace of blood or tissue anywhere on the property. Kennedy must have chopped her up somewhere else."

Sweede slammed his note pad on the desk. "I don't buy it. Why would Kennedy chop her up in one place and bring the bloodied murder weapon back to the house? That whole place is spotless. He's got a cleaning business, for Christ's sake."

With a wave of his hand, Chung dismissed the comment. "That's for the DA to figure out."

"Like hell it is! Did the DA figure out a motive yet? The others have motives too! It's called money! Judy Kennedy's life insurance was only worth fifty grand. The investigation has just started. The DA jumped the gun and you jumped in with him!"

Chung stared at his paperwork and took a deep breath. "Sweede, the evidence points to Will Kennedy. The press is all over this. Judy Kennedy is having her fifteen minutes of fame. A picture of her hand is on the damn Internet!

"If you have more, I want to hear it. Until then, we need to move on - we've got a lot of ground to cover. Let's start with Ginger Stoolman's disappearance and what's happening at the bank. By the way, Alfred Locke had a massive stroke or something. He's on life support."

Sweede whistled sharply. "I knew it! You should have seen his coloring. He was as white as sheet and sweating like a pig! He went down like a ton of bricks!"

Ted squirmed in his seat.

"What's wrong with you?" Sweede asked with a snicker.

"I hate talking about strokes or heart attacks. Now, my ass is quivering! It's stress!"

Sweede laughed. "Have a couple of beers. That'll stop the quivering."

"All right, all right, we've got our own stress. I hope Locke hangs in there. We need him. If he's involved in any of this mess, he'll crack," Chung noted as he jerked at his bowtie.

Smirking, Sweede turned to Ted. "I'd say he already cracked!"

Chung reproached Sweede. "You said that Ginger Stoolman stated that Judy Kennedy bribed Locke. He may be in deeper than we think. It may have been more than just porno pictures that he was afraid of.

"That Freddy sounds pretty wacky; does he fit in?

"If Ginger is telling the truth about Judy embezzling money from Locke and then Judy turning on her, then you're right: they both have a motive for killing her.

"So where's Ginger? Is she dead or did she just take off to save her own ass? Would her disappearance benefit Locke or Will Kennedy?

"Did she help Locke embezzle the money, and then try to extort more or threaten him with disclosure? Maybe it was the other way around.

"Locke could have dumped the blame on both Ginger and Judy to save himself. He's no fool. He's got more to lose than anyone.

"You know, Locke said that he played racquetball and did some swimming with Kennedy. I wouldn't be surprised if Judy, Will, and Locke were in it together. Will Kennedy is somewhere in the embezzlement mix!

"For now, you guys are going to arrest him for the murder of his wife. We have a statement from Judy's bank buddy, the bird-watching park ranger who saw them fighting around the time she disappeared.

"We did find that suitcase he talked about. There was no money it. We have the saw blade with blood and body tissue on it, and strands of Judy's hair and pieces of her scalp, a DNA match. Her cell and pocketbook were found at the bottom of the pond behind their house.

"Now go pick him up!"

CHAPTER TWENTY THREE

The familiar sound of Alice White's husky voice comforted Charlie's clients. "Good afternoon, Attorney Charles Sudanski's office."

"Hi, Alice, how are you? It's Will, Will Kennedy.

"Thanks, Alice. Yeah, it's turned into what I thought it would. They arrested me a couple of hours ago.

"Have Charlie come over as soon as he can. I'm here in Suffolk.

"I know you do, Alice, and I appreciate it. You're right; the husband is always the number-one suspect."

Under the eye-throbbing glare of fluorescent lights, a guard hustled Will through long, gray, cinderblock corridors. His road ahead began with the clang and lock of the door behind him. He rested on a small cot while listening to the chatter and murmuring that echoed around him - whispered words of rumor and testimony, empty oaths, and hollow dreams that mark the days and nights of every inmate.

A booming voice jolted Kennedy from his sleep. "Hey, Kennedy, get up, you've got a visitor. Let's go, let's go. I haven't got all day. Hurry up, your lawyer's waiting for you in the conference room downstairs."

Charles Sudanski threw his briefcase on a table and laughed. "Willy boy, this is like the old days. Last time we did this routine, you were in Charles Street. How long ago was that - twenty-five, thirty years? I got a few years knocked off of your sentence too," he prattled while sorting his paperwork.

Will humored Sudanski and let him break the ice before they turned to business.

The former marine still sported a crew-cut. Unlike the gray-suited tribe of his profession, Charlie wore over his powerful frame a trademark, impeccably tailored, navy blue sport coat and gray slacks. Sudanski was built like an armored tank and moved through the legal system in just that way.

"Still don't show your cards, huh, Will? No one ever sees you sweat!"

Kennedy raised his brows, nodded his head slightly, and smiled at his friend.

Sudanski clicked his tongue. "I told you not to marry her but never thought you'd wind up wearing that outfit because of it. You look more comfortable in your sweats running up and down G Street. You'll be back there pronto.

"The evidence is piling up, but we can work through it. First of all, you know the drill: don't talk to anyone but me, Mercer, or my new associate, Christine O'Malley."

Will's face clouded. "I thought Mercer was gone?"

"You know how it is. He's my sister's kid. I've kept him on longer than I've wanted to, but the booze is really getting to him. He knows his days are numbered with me. He's looking for another job.

"And now, my sister knows it, so she isn't speaking to me! I hired Christine about a year ago. She's a smart cookie. You'll like her. While I'm on vacation, you'll be speaking with either one of them, most likely with Christine, if Mercer's in court."

Will crossed his arms over his chest. "Christ, Charlie, do you have to go on vacation now?"

"Look, we've been friends for a long time. If my daughter weren't getting married in frigging Australia, I'd be here. I have no choice."

"Oh, sorry. I understand. Congratulations. But I don't want that lush Mercer near me, and I don't even know this Christine!"

"Will, Christine O'Malley is a crackerjack. I'd let her defend me. She knows what she's doing."

"What's her background? How much experience does she have? Charlie, don't stick me with some rookie."

Sudanski leaned forward with his palms spread. "Will, do you have to break my balls? I'm telling you, she's a class act. She knows what she's doing. What do you want, her damn resume?"

"It's not a bad idea."

"Oh, cut the crap, Will!"

"Charlie, you're not the one stuck in this dump. And I want a call from you every day, every damn day!"

Sudanski unbuttoned his sport coat and loosened his tie. "If that's what you want, Will, then that's what you've got. We'll do it your way. I'll have Mercer work in the background, and I'll check in with you every day.

"But you've got to see Mercer once. I've already got it scheduled. Christine is in court the day after tomorrow, and we've got to move on this. If something comes up unexpectedly, call me on my cell, day or night. Just remember the time difference.

"Is it all right if we get down to business now, or do you want to yank my chain a little more? For the good guy you turned out to be, you can still be a pain in the ass!"

Will nodded.

Sudanski slid off the cap of his sleek silver pen and straightened the yellow legal pad before him. He adjusted his gleaming gold cufflinks, artfully engraved with the U.S. Marine insignia and made a quick notation on the legal pad. "Will, just listen before you say anything. Their evidence is compelling.

"Here's what I got from the DA: Judy told you she was going to Atlanta on bank business and then to Florida to meet her girlfriends. She doesn't return home when she's supposed to. You report her missing the next day. The bank knows nothing of any trip to Atlanta. She told three different stories, to three different people, about where she was going.

"The day after that, a kid in Scituate is pulling lobster traps with her father. They find a severed hand caught in the netting. The wedding band is still on it and has both your initials engraved on the inside.

"Detectives Swenson and Smith pay you a visit and give you the bad news. You identify the rings from a photo and give them Judy's hair brush for DNA testing."

Sudanski glanced away from his notes. "I know your marriage was on the rocks for a long time, Will, but was it that bad? I'm not sensing much grief."

Kennedy ran his hand through his hair, suspecting what Sudanski was thinking: would a jury understand?

"Charlie," he said firmly, "I'm not going to act like some grieving husband that I'm not. There was nothing between us for years, since Jamie died. I stayed with her because I felt guilty about his death, plus the fact that she couldn't carry another baby full term. She miscarried four times.

"I felt sorry for her. I tried to help her for years. You know that," he protested, his voice rising in frustration. "Judy was mentally ill but smart enough to control me with her blame game, and I fell for it. But not anymore.

"In the end, we couldn't stand the sight of each other." Dropping his face in his hands, Will added, "You'll have to find a way around that."

Sudanski gently laid down his pen. "Will, I've known you for a long time. I never believed she was the right person for you. Your self-esteem was low, but hers was lower. And you never took off those rose-colored glasses.

"And now you're paying for it. But you can't pay for it by giving another twenty-five years to life. If this goes to trial, you need to show some remorse. Help me out, for Christ's sake."

"What you're saying may be true, but don't try to make me out to be something I'm not! I'm sorry for the way she lived, and I'm sorry for the way she died, but I'm not sorry she's out of my life. I didn't kill her. And I don't know who did. I hope that whatever she couldn't find here she finds in some afterlife - if there is one."

Sudanski studied his client. "Parochial school left a bad taste in all our mouths, but I get it - and now you need to get it! You've done your time in hell living with her, but you can't give any more because of her. That's all I'm saying. Don't shoot yourself in the foot. Don't be so damn stubborn!"

He shook his head in exasperation. "Look, just think about it, will you? Just think about it!"

Kennedy knew Sudanski was right. "All right, Charlie. I'll think about it."

The attorney heaved a sigh of relief. "Good. Now look, I think we've got enough to raise more than a reasonable doubt, if this goes to trial. Judy was a busy girl, had a lot going on that I'm sure you didn't know about."

"That's for sure."

Sudanski returned to his notes. "Where were we? Here we are.

"So you gave the hairbrush to the detectives for DNA samples. You're shown the ring and identify it."

Sudanski leaned over and placed a hand on Kennedy's shoulder. "Will, Judy's death was pretty gruesome. I'm not making light of it. I'm just dealing with the facts as I got them from the DA."

"I know, go ahead."

"The hand was severed at the wrist, so they figure she was dismembered with a saw and dumped in the bay. Pieces of her scalp and hair clogged the sea strainer of Detective Swenson's boat."

Will's jaw dropped. "Are you kidding me? Judy's hair screwed up his engine?"

"Engine*s*," said Sudanski. "Dual inboard engines, brand damn new! Stranger things have happened, Will, but this is pretty damn unbelievable."

He laughed hardily "It's one for the books!"

The lawyer skimmed through the details of his documents. "Okay, so they interview people at the bank and find out Judy was no bargain, had a lousy reputation, and was having a love affair with Ginger Stoolman, who dumped her.

"Did they show you any photos of Judy and Ginger? Do you know this Ginger?"

"I met her a few times at bank functions, holiday parties, that kind of stuff. And, yes, I saw the photos. The cops showed them to me."

Sudanski searched Will's face, and spoke cautiously. "I just found out that this Ginger is missing. Do you know anything about it? Have you had any recent conversations or meetings with her, any type of correspondence?"

Kennedy closed his eyes and shook his head. "No."

"Judy was also having an affair with a Freddy Nunn. Did you know about that?"

Will stammered in disbelief. "No, I, - God Almighty, Charlie, the detective mentioned that to me. I thought he was lying, just trying to break my balls. I can't believe that she was shacking up with him too! I helped that kid out!"

"What do you mean?"

"I helped him build a new set of back stairs, took down a few dead trees in his back yard - stuff like that. Judy was over there a few times a week. She said he was adopted. After his mother died, she spent a lot of time helping him find his real mother or something like that. That's what she told me anyway. Who the hell knows?"

Sudanski's face brightened. "Let's go back to the stairs you built and the dead trees. Who owned the saws, you or Freddy?"

"I used my own saws."

"Hmm," he murmured. "This Freddy says that he saw you and Judy brawling out in front of your house. He says that you smacked her around, pulled a suitcase full of money out of her hand, shoved her into the car, and took off with her crying."

"It never happened."

Sudanski scribbled a few words and underlined them. "The detectives return and find a bloody saw blade on one visit. Judy's cell and pocketbook are found in the bottom of the pond out back of your place. They do some background checks and find your rap sheet from thirty years ago and a charge of assault and battery Judy filed against you last year. She never followed up on it."

Kennedy's face reddened. "I never hit her. I wouldn't hit a woman, period. And I don't know how blood got on any of my saw blades or how Judy's cell or pocketbook got to the bottom of the pond. I'm telling you, Charlie, I'm being set-up."

"By whom and why?"

Will slumped into his chair and shrugged his shoulders. "I don't know. I just don't know."

"Give me something to go on Will!"

He dropped his head into his hands. "I don't have anything for you to go on. And don't you start doubting me."

Sudanski leaned back and ran his fingers between the collar of his shirt and neck. "Will, I'm just playing the devil's advocate here."

"I know you are, but you need to find a way around this," he pleaded. "But this stuff just keeps piling up. I hate being trapped like some animal in this dump!"

"We'll get it straightened out, Will. I just need a little time - a little more information. Things are unfolding at the bank. There may be a connection."

Kennedy glanced at the gray walls around him. "All right, Charlie, all right. Finish with what you were saying."

Sudanski breathed deep. "It's my understanding that the bank's missing a ton of money - almost a million and a half. The examiners are in. It looks like Judy had her hand in the till. But they need more time to prove it.

"Alfred Locke implied that you might have something to do with it. I'm wondering if he had something to do with it. What have you got to say for yourself?"

"Alfred Locke said I might have something to do with missing money? Are you sure? I don't believe it!"

Sudanski nodded. "That's what the DA says. That's what I was told."

"Well, you were told wrong. That's nothing but bullshit!"

"Why would Alfred Locke say it, if there wasn't some truth to it?"

"He'd say it to cover his own ass!" snapped Will.

Sudanski rapidly rubbed his palms together. "Ah, things are heating up! This guy, Alfred Locke, says that you and he played racquetball and a little golf together once in a while, and that you swim at the same club, is that right?"

"Yeah, that's right."

"He also said that he told you that Judy was taking out personal loans and telling you that they were bonuses. Is that right? You thought they were bonuses?"

"Yeah, the bonus part is right, but he didn't say anything about any loans."

Sudanski looked over Locke's deposition and nodded. "Well, Judy was telling you that those checks were bonuses when, in fact, they were personal loans. She'd take them out and pay them back a couple of months later - more of her lying, puffing herself up, more fuel for us."

"Well, I fell for it!"

"You sure did fall for it. Oh, and by the way, this Alfred Locke had a stroke or something. The DA says he's on life support. They're hoping he'll pull through so they can finish questioning him. And with Ginger Stoolman missing, they can't follow-up and question her again. So, we may have missing links that we need to work around."

Kennedy sighed. "Any more good news?"

"No, that just about wraps it up. Can you account for your whereabouts each and every day that Judy was missing?"

"I'll just check my work schedule. I was covering for vacations and worked out before and after work, every day, like I always do, and at the same places. If there's anyone who saw me, but doesn't remember, Big Brother will. There are cameras everywhere."

"That's for sure, not a bad thing in a case like this," Sudanski said, tapping his pen against the table. "We'll soon find out. We've got a lot to do. And for Christ's sake, don't worry; you're going to be all right."

He glanced at the clock. "I'm running late!"

The attorney gathered the paperwork and handed Will the pen. "Sign here, here, and here, and, on this one, I need your signature and date."

Kennedy signed and slid the papers to Sudanski, who stood to stretch his aching back. He shut his briefcase and placed a strong hand firmly on Will's shoulder.

"Now don't forget, Christine will see you in a few days. I'll see you in a week, and we'll talk every day. Look, I've got to get going. Got to pick up my dog and bring him to the kennel while Marie and I are away."

Sudanski stood holding his briefcase and jingling change in his pocket. "Can I do anything for you before I go?"

"Let me use your pen again." Will carefully wrote a name and number and handed it to his defense attorney. "Call my crew manager. Ask him to check on the house and to give you a key so you can get in."

Sudanski scanned the note and shoved it in his pocket. "We're going to get you out of this, but you've got homework to do. Start writing a log of who you talked with and where you were since the last time you saw Judy. It's one of the first things Christine O'Malley will be looking for."

"Okay, Charlie, I got it."

The lawyer gave him a firm slap on the back. "All right, see you in a week or so, after the wedding."

"Congratulations, Charlie. Give my best to Marie and your daughter. Have a good trip!"

CHAPTER TWENTY FOUR

Marybeth Murphy's vacation plans were ruined. The microburst had taken out the old elm, and it lay hazardously tipped atop the garage, its long, splintered branches jutting out over the roof. "Gillan, we'll never get to Bar Harbor," she moaned.

"Yes we will. I've got to go and follow-up on where I left off last night." He pecked her on the cheek and hastily left with an edgy Ronan.

The neighborhood looked like a damn tornado hit. Branches, barrels, trees, and shingles, littered the land. Utility trucks cautiously maneuvered around the mess and dump trucks and front-end loaders clearing and cleaning the sidewalks and streets. City workers called and waved to Gillan as he sprinted behind Ronan, moving away from the chaos and racket around them.

Ronan paused for a split second, lifted his head to sniff the air above and around him, and eagerly drew in the scent. His frantic sense for the blue tug toy electrified every muscle in his quivering body. As his intensity swelled, Gillan watched the dog's head move lower to the ground, his twitching ears pricked forward and black muzzle moving in a spasmodic frenzy, sniffing deep into the damp grass.

They made good time. The tide was out, so the marsh was dry and the reeds, tall and stiff. Gillan dodged them and moved to the shore line hastily stumbling over the rocks that marked a granite incline.

He jerked the dog's leash. "Halt." Gillan stopped and looked at the rocky incline and moaned. "That hill's a friggin' hundred feet up!"

Panting and drooling, Ronan followed Gillan's eyes to the top of a stony ledge. He yapped and whined impatiently, scanning the rocky terrain and his handler's face. "All right, Ronan, let's go. Find."

Man and dog lurched forward, up and over the rugged terrain above the beach. After fifty feet, they stopped at a flat, jutting rock from which Gillan could see the bay's dark and choppy water.

Gillan wiped sweat from his face, opened his gear pack, and poured water into a thermos. Ronan slurped it and looked with expectation at Gillan. It was time to move.

The two climbed cautiously and mounted the rocky ridge. A damp, leafy footpath, ripe with the fragrance of wet earth, wild berries, and milkweed opened to a huge clearing of soft summer grass that shimmered bright and emerald green in the late-morning sun. They had arrived in somebody's back yard.

Ronan's glistening eyes fixed on a grassy knoll.

Gillan looked around in amazement. "We're in luck. The storm didn't touch this place!" With no one nearby, it was almost too quiet. Gillan followed the dog's stare to a soft depression on the far side of the yard. Ronan stood panting and pulled forward.

Gillian tugged the leash. "Sit."

His curiosity mounted, and he moved ahead. If the owners asked, he was just taking a short cut. He looked down at his dog. "Find!"

Ronan rushed onward, nose to the ground, tracking the scent, his slender body jolting and shifting left to right. He swiftly moved to the shallow depression, buried his nose there, barked once, and sat with certainty.

"Good boy, good boy. Do you want your tug toy, huh? Do you want your blue toy?" Ronan jumped and frolicked in dizzying circles around his handler. Gillan whipped the blue tug toy across the yard, and Ronan tore after it, made a great leap, dashed back to Gillan, and dropped the toy at his feet.

Briskly rubbing his dog's fine, black head and ears he dangled the toy before his eyes again. Ronan wrestled it from him, and then playfully jaunted around, taunting his handler to take it.

He struggled for the toy but surrendered it to the handsome shepherd. Ronan lay down in the shade, softly chewing his reward.

Gillan crouched over the shallow depression and, with his fingers, stirred the sandy soil, and felt a smooth, round object. From his gear pack, he pulled a tiny brush and plastic gloves and dusted the sandy soil away from the object.

The sun flashed across a brilliant metal surface of a button, a silver button. He fished a pencil and camera from his gear pack and took shots of the silver button with the pencil alongside.

"It hasn't been here long, Ronan. No rust or corrosion, no imbedded soil."

He dug deeper and extracted a shell casing, probably a .38. He laid the pencil beside it and clicked the camera.

Warily, the detective looked around the scene and dropped the button and shell casing into a plastic bag.

"Ronan!"

He ignored his handler and continued gnawing the toy.

"Drop it."

Ronan paused but dropped the blue toy. Gillan leashed him a good twenty feet away from the depression in the sand.

"Find." Ronan confidently trotted to the shallow depression.

"No," said Gillan, sweeping his arm toward the great white house. "Find."

Ronan nuzzled the grass and snaked forward, inhaling and sniffing the ground that led to the house. His firm auburn tail furiously sweeping side to side, he looked quizzically at Gillan.

"Nothing left for you here, Ronan? Okay."

He pulled out his cell. "Mars, its Gillan."

"Hey, Gillan, doing any fishing?"

"Not since Sweede's engines blew on our last trip out."

"Did he ever find out what happened?"

"Oh, yeah, would you believe the sea strainer was clogged with hair, bone and scalp tissue?"

"You're kidding!"

"Nope, and get this: it was a DNA match to some lady whose husband reported her missing to Sweede a couple of days before!"

"Is that right? We ought to write a book. I just pulled some guy from a lake up here. He was stabbed in his cottage, dragged to his boat, chained to a cinderblock, and dumped. Tonto tracked it all down. I'm telling you Gillan, he's the best cadaver-sniffer I've ever had."

"I know, Mars. That's what I'm calling about. Any chance you can bring him down here? Ronan picked up a gunpowder scent, and we followed it from my house. Good thing the wind was blowing from the right direction. Anyway, we found a button and a shell casing. If there's a cadaver or any tissue around, Tonto will find it."

"I'm off tomorrow, Gillan. I'll see you about ten. If there's something there, you're right, we'll find it!"

CHAPTER TWENTY FIVE

The deafening sound of the breakfast bell exploded in Will Kennedy's ears, and he jolted upright in his bed. "Another day in paradise," he thought, dropping into his pillow.

Once in the noisy chow line, he felt heavy and vague and slowly moved for a cup of coffee and cornflakes.

"Is this your first time in?"

Will turned and faced a grinning, rotting-toothed kid, his stringy brown hair nearly covering his eyes.

"You're in luck! Today, we're having bagels, and every Sunday, we have scrambled eggs and bacon!"

Kennedy returned the grin. "As long as there are prisons, there'll be coffee, cornflakes, and bagels, and on Sundays, bacon and scrambled eggs."

The kid wiped a strand of hair from his eyes and picked up a tray. "It's better than what I eat outside of here. At least I have a roof over my head and three squares a day."

Will sat away from the noise of the cafeteria, sipping a cup of black coffee. He finished quickly and escaped to the safety and solitude of his cell, away from reminders of his used-to-be life.

Following Sudanski's direction, Will methodically recorded every movement he could recall since Judy's disappearance. He ate a tuna sandwich for lunch and reread his unremarkable chronicle: the same thing, day after long day, work, run, swim, and read. If Judy were alive, the story would not have changed.

Kennedy fought the sense of bleakness that seemed to circle like vultures above or starved street dogs below nipping at his heels. He grabbed his pencil, wrote in bold, block letters on the cover of his notebook, *My Way Out*, and lay on his cot to await the arrival of Christine O'Malley, his lawyer of the week.

He liked the name, Christine, ever since he met Christine Marie Sandonato.

They were just kids and crazy about each other - but nothing like puppy love. She had given up on him and moved on.

Still, Kennedy thought about her every once in a while, knowing that in one way or another, he had loved her his whole life. Will could not remember their parting but knew its cause: he neglected her and spent more time in places like jail than with that beautiful, sensitive thing of intelligence that made up her being.

The guard's bark punctured his thoughts. "Kennedy, your lawyer is downstairs. Let's go."

Upon entering the conference area, Will stopped short at the sight of Sudanski's secretary. "Alice, what are you doing here?"

She rolled her eyes and spoke in her deep, gravelly voice. "Everyone is in court, and Sudanski called. He'll call you later. He told me to stop by and be sure that you're working on your journal. He wants a good chunk of it done by tomorrow, so we can start working on it.

"He knew you didn't want Mercer here anyway, but, tomorrow, he and Christine are going to your house. They'll be looking at your insurance policies and taking photographs of your house and yard and all that stuff. The cops have already been there. Where do you keep the insurance policies?"

"Everything is up in my study. There's a desk up there; the policies are in the bottom draw. I have a safe deposit box at the Shore Bank with my will and some other paperwork in it, but you have copies of most of the stuff that's in there."

Alice nodded and sat down. "They're laying the foundation for your case, so Christine O'Malley will be here to see you tomorrow afternoon. I'm sure she'll have a million more questions. She always does."

Alice had known Kennedy since he was a screwed up kid but admired how he had pulled himself together. "Can I do anything for you, Will?"

"No, but I appreciate you coming by."

"You've had a lot of company. I passed your sisters when I was coming in. I'm glad you have the support you should have at a time like this. But, you'll be out of here in no time, so try not to worry. You've got a friend in Charlie Sudanski; he's the best criminal defense lawyer in Boston."

"You're right. Thanks Alice."

CHAPTER TWENTY SIX

Marybeth was certain that Mars Starr would be a perfect match for her best friend. French and half-Black Foot Indian, Mars stood big and brawny, all muscle, and, in the summer, as brown as a Boston Baked Bean.

His sociable smile flashed a perfect set of white teeth, and he winked at Gillan as they watched Marybeth flutter around the kitchen placing steaming waffles on their plates and piling on fresh strawberries. Like a flamboyant musical conductor who brings a rousing close to a great symphony, she scooped a lavish portion of sweet whipped cream and plunked it with gusto atop the succulent fruit.

Mars grinned and looked at her. "Marybeth, do you have a twin?"

"No, but I have a friend who's a close second. I could send her up to your cabin to braid your ponytail. She'll want to know how you got a name like Mars Starr."

"I never met my father, and my mother was shaman of her tribe up in Ottawa, and a pot-smoking astrologer. You can take it from there." He picked up his fork and knife and carefully cut into his waffles.

Marybeth blushed and finished drying the mixing bowl. "I'm sorry, Mars. I didn't mean to pry."

He smiled broadly. "It's just part of who I am, Marybeth. I'm happy in my own skin. And these waffles are delicious."

She breathed a sigh of relief and put the bowl away.

Mars and Gillan gathered their gear, leashed their dogs, and left. Gillan pulled out the silver button and shell casing. "Ronan smelled gunpowder, and here's what I found."

Donning his gloves, Mars examined the findings. "Do we have a search warrant?"

"Not yet. Wanted to see what you think. If anyone asks, we're just a couple of handlers walking our dogs."

They mounted the harsh, rocky incline, ducked below hanging vines, and dodged springing branches along a narrow pathway that led to the yard. Tonto held his head high in the air, tugged at his leash, and yelped.

Mars scanned the yard. "There's something here, for sure."

Tonto looked at him puzzled.

He squatted and stared into the dog's luminous brown eyes and gently touched his moist black nose. "Okay, my friend, it's all yours. Find!"

Tonto leapt ahead and plunged his black muzzle to the ground. He zigzagged feverishly along the edge of the yard, past the overgrowth of shrubs, weeds, and berry-laden bushes, circled the shallow depression, sat, and gave a short, sharp bark.

"Is that where you picked up the shell casing and button?"

Gillan nodded. "Yeah, that's exactly where I found them."

Mars crouched and examined some soil.

"Something here was oozing blood. There's some body tissue here, too. Good boy, Tonto."

Mars ran his hand over the shepherd's back. "Look what I've got," he said, dangling a soft, red tug toy before him.

Tonto franticly tugged and yanked it from Mars's grip and pranced around him, furiously shaking the toy.

"Drop it."

Tonto stared at his handler, the toy dangling from his mouth. Mars stared straight back.

"Drop it."

He let the toy drop and sat panting, pink tongue lolling, and shifting his chocolate- colored eyes from the toy that lay before him, to his handler standing over him.

Tonto followed Mars' gaze to the great white house that lay in the distance. "Looks pretty clear. Let's go."

The dog's ears flicked forward, and he stood up waiting for his master's command, "Tonto, find."

The strapping shepherd pulled ahead. He and Mars shifted from the shade and into the sunlight, moving cross-wise over the yard. While Tonto sniffed furiously, Mars sprinted behind him, studying the grass.

"Hold," he commanded. Tonto stopped dead in his tracks.

Mars crouched and pointed to a bright blue article in the grass. "Gillan, what's a nose clip doing here?"

He quickly joined Mars and hastily pulled out his camera, pencil, and a plastic bag. "Let me get a few shots and bag it."

Starr stood up and looked around. "Gillan, take a few shots of that, too," he said, pointing to a drag trail from the shallow depression where the grass lay flat and led to the sidewalk.

Tonto tugged on his leash, and Mars gave the command and followed. The dog sat and barked once.

"Take a look at this Gillan," he remarked pointing to divots in the soil. "More tissue, more blood, and hair. A few strands of it are mixed in with the grass."

Mars Starr looked at the bright, blue sky and the clumps of grass and hair in his hand. "You're right, Gillan. It sure seems like something went down here."

CHAPTER TWENTY SEVEN

G illan sauntered through the bustling office of his police barracks and rapped on Captain Chung's door. "Come in, come in," he bawled, annoyed at the interruption to his lunch.

With Gillan in tow, Ronan poked his black nose between the slender door opening and scampered into Chung's office.

"I thought you were on vacation, and I told you not to bring that dog in here."

Ronan stared at Chung and then his handler, who said, "I'm on vacation, but I need a search warrant."

"Then you're not on vacation, and you have to change your time."

Chung poked a tomato slice into his sandwich. "Well, go ahead. Don't let my lunch stop you. Why do you need a search warrant? I'm busy. I've got paperwork up the ying-yang.

"Alfred Locke was taken off that breathing machine. They think he might pull through. Ginger Stoolman is still missing.

"Sweede and Ted arrested Will Kennedy, and I've got half the squad up in Dorchester with a bank holdup and the other half breaking up a damn prostitution ring at that shithole of a massage parlor on the corner of Beale Street and Newport Avenue.

"Now, why do you need a search warrant?"

"Ronan detected gunpowder the other night. I followed him to his mark and found a button and shell casing in a shallow grave. Mars brought Tonto up there this morning. They found blood, body tissue, and a few hair samples on a drag track. And they found a nose clip."

"A nose clip?"

"Yeah, swimmers use them."

Chung swallowed a bite of his sandwich and washed it down with ginger ale. "The homeowners might be swimmers. Did they invite you in to search their property? They must be nice people."

Gillan tilted his head and shrugged his shoulders. "Mars and I were just two guys out walking our dogs. I found out that the property belongs to Freddy Nunn. There may be a connection to the Kennedy case. And Will Kennedy is a quite a swimmer.

"I did some checking on him, too. He placed fifth in that Boston and the Islands relay race this past July. His groupies think that he's some kind of righteous dude."

"Where's the button and shell casing and the bloody grass and soil? Where's the nose clip?"

"Everything is bagged and downstairs, going to forensics and ballistics. We need that search warrant."

Chung squeezed the sandwich wrapper into a ball, tossed it into the trash, then carefully un-wrapped his brownies.

"It's shaky Gillan, it's shaky. Maybe the homeowner was a nose-clipped swimmer shooting at squirrels. Maybe the damn squirrels were wearing nose clips! The button could have fallen off anyone's jacket!"

Chung checked his watch. "Look, I've got a meeting. I'll check with the DA's office. Call me after three."

CHAPTER TWENTY EIGHT

B y 3:30, Christine O'Malley was running late. She had not read Kennedy's deposition, missed lunch, and had to drive across town to pick up her clothes at the cleaners, then, make it to the jail by four. She wanted to be on time for dinner with Dan Robbins, a colleague and her first date since her husband Jeffrey's death.

Christine bit into a piece of dark chocolate and let it melt in her mouth, waited for a light to change, but no one moved when it turned green. The intersection was blocked.

Piercing screams of sirens came from behind her, so she turned down the radio and checked her rearview mirror. Cars and trucks nudged and jerked away from oncoming squad cars with blue lights flashing and ambulances.

Christine followed suit. The caravan whizzed by and stopped on Washington Street, a few blocks up. "Oh no," she moaned. "I'm trapped! I'll be here until midnight." It was nearly five when she pulled into the jail parking lot and hurried up the steps.

The guard watched with pleasure as she approached. "You're late for a Friday, Christine."

"Am I ever. I've been out straight all day! There's a fire on Washington Street, near the hospital."

"Who are you here to see?"

She squinted at the name on the folder. "Wilbur Kenney, no, William, William H. Kenney. I'm sorry, I better find my glasses. I haven't had time to go over this guy's case yet. Mercer was supposed to take it on, but he's too busy. I just picked it up this afternoon."

He checked a roster. "Do you mean William X. Kennedy?"

Christine peered through her glasses at the name on the folder. "Yes, that's it. William Kennedy."

"Boston is full of them!" he said.

"That's for sure!"

"I'll have him brought downstairs. Come on Christine, I'll walk you down there."

Attorney and jailer chatted as they walked along the long corridors and past yellowed wall postings asking for AIDS research volunteers, the benefits of proper hand washing techniques, how to practice safe sex, and prisoners' rights.

Kennedy heard their approaching footsteps and guessed it was a woman by the lightness of the steps. The other must be an overweight guard, plodding along, his raspy voice griping about something.

He listened intently. There was something about the woman's voice that caught his attention. It was distinct, throaty, and melodic.

The burly guard unlocked the door, and she briskly stepped inside the dismal meeting room. Will was stunned but caught the whole scene in a split second: shining black hair, creamy skin on mile-high cheekbones, a cleft in her chin, and the most expressive brown eyes he had ever seen.

Nothing about her had changed. The only person in his life whom he respected and trusted, who had lit in his soul an undying flame of passion and tenderness - Christine Marie Sandonato - was walking towards him.

Will turned to the wall.

Extending her hand to him, she inquired, "Mr. Kennedy, William Kennedy?"

He slowly slid his hand from his forehead and turned to face her, his heart pounding.

Their eyes locked in amazement, and her briefcase dropped to the floor.

"Will! Will, I had no idea. I didn't make the connection."

Memories of him flooded her mind and returned her to a time when she loved him with every breath of her being. Now, no sense of time or the passing years remained, no feeling of grief, pain, or separation, only wonderment.

Christine brought her trembling hand to her forehead and struggled to find something to say. "My sister Natalie and I were just speaking about you. I told her I never knew what happened to you."

Will blushed and lowered his eyes.

Christine searched for the right words. "Oh, I'm sorry. I didn't mean it that way. It's been a long time Will," she heard herself mumble.

Her legs shaking, she pulled up a chair and sat beside him. "It's quite a shock to see you and, you're in quite a jam. I'm so sorry that after all this time we need to meet under these circumstances," she sighed.

"It's just that, it's awkward for both of us. You can call Charlie if you want. You have the right to ask for someone else. I know you don't want Mercer in here. Charlie won't be back for a week, but his brother has a practice, and he could fill in."

Will looked at her. "Christine, I didn't kill my wife. And you can stay. It's good to see you."

She nervously brushed the hair away from her face. "Okay, if you say so. You can change your mind at any time."

He nodded and smiled. "How have you been?"

"Okay. Life has taken some twists and turns, but I guess that's what it's all about."

Christine looked away from him and surveyed the room with its concrete walls and orange plastic chairs.

She smiled shyly. "At least I'm not in jail," she quipped, "and you are!"

"That's right," he laughed, "but not for long I hope. Are your legal skills as good as your sense of humor? I hope that you're good at this."

Christine felt her body relax. "You haven't lost your sense of humor either, Will."

She blushed and beamed at him. "Charlie will be back before you know it. In the meantime, we have a lot of work to do."

Attorney and accused sat under the bleak lights and unyielding walls around them, speaking quietly, Christine taking notes, questioning him, and clarifying his answers.

The jailer's voice interrupted. "Closing time; you have ten minutes."

"Yes, thank you. We're just finishing up."

A bittersweet smile crossed her lips. "Where does the time go?"

"Christine, I haven't had a drink in almost thirty years."

She searched his eyes, still glittering like emeralds in the sun.

"I'm really happy for you, Will. I'm proud of you. I know it must have taken a lot of courage," she said quietly.

"Charlie Sudanski is your biggest supporter and the best lawyer around. You two have known each other for years, and he's a good judge of character. You have a lot working in your favor."

His lover of yesteryear drew closer to him and spoke in hushed tones, like a mother whose soothing words and gentle hands bring comfort to a feverish child.

"You've got two minutes," warned the guard.

She pressed the black attaché to her chest. "Well, time to go. I've got my work cut out for the weekend."

Will caught a glint of tears in her eyes. There was so much he wanted to say, but was afraid to - afraid it would come out all wrong. Words swirled in his head, *Don't leave, don't go!* He took a deep breath. "Hey, Christine," he blurted, "is your mother still with us? Is she still alive?"

Stunned, she recalled her mother's dislike of him and stood in silence before laughing. "Yes, yes, she is, Will. Rose is still alive and kicking! And the older she gets, the harder she kicks. It just doesn't hurt as much."

His face brightened. "Your father should have bought her a football!"

"My father was her football!"

A smug smile crossed his face. "Well, tell her I said, 'Hello.' "

"I'll do that Will, when your defense team gets you out of jail. I wouldn't give her the satisfaction of knowing that history repeats itself, and that she was right about you all along!"

Will flushed but burst into a broad grin. "She was right the first time, but not this time!"

He saw the gleam in Christine's eyes and felt warm and good because of it. Will watched her walk away and sensed a sudden burn of tears in his eyes.

Christine's radiance had filled the room and touched every part of his being with a sense of joy he forgot had existed.

Kennedy walked to his cell wondering, "Who's the lucky guy she's going home to?"

CHAPTER TWENTY NINE

Rather than her usual route home, Christine moved slowly through the early evening traffic heading to South Boston, passed the triple-decker where Will grew up, turned onto East Broadway and right at G Street. She slowed and parked in front of the high school.

The day's sun had dropped to the horizon and, with its descent, painted the evening sky in glowing shades of rosy reds, pinks, and lavenders. She sat watching the kids laughing, talking, holding hands, and making their way to Thomas Park, like she and Will had done so many years ago.

God! How she had loved him but never fit into his life.

Kennedy and Judy were another story, at least for a while. She assumed his bad boy days and the twists and turns in their lives had taken a toll. Her days of asking why life unfolded as it did were far behind.

Done reminiscing, Christine started her car and drove home preoccupied with thoughts of Will sitting in a jail cell, unsure whether he was innocent of murdering Judy or simply wanting to believe it.

She unlocked the front door to rooms dark and quiet. Her muscles ached and her head throbbed. Christine felt emotionally drained and needed a good cry. She dropped her attaché in the hallway before staring miserably into the empty refrigerator, opened a jar of peanut butter, made a sandwich, filled a glass with wine, settled into her easy chair, and wept.

Christine cried for herself, for everything that had gone so hideously and heartbreakingly wrong, for Will, and about him. She wept about their short life together, always interrupted, but felt thankful that memories of him had remained tenderly in her heart for all these years.

She sobbed about Jeffrey's death, his charades, her stupidity, his lies, her delusions that what they had would last forever weighed on her. She sat silent for a long time, blew her nose, dried her eyes, and attempted to read Will's deposition. Unable to concentrate, she returned it to its folder.

Phone messages needed answers. Dan had waited at Louie's for her until seven. Better to call him in the morning and apologize.

With effort, she undressed, changed into her robe, filled the tub, and sat on its edge, watching the crystal blue mineral salts dissolve into the steaming bathwater. Christine eased into the tub, closed her eyes, and sighed with relief, her body still, the temple of her thoughts quiet.

Somewhere she had read that love is as perennial as the grass - a good thought, if true.

•••

With a book on his lap and his back against the wall, Kennedy sat on his jail cot thinking about Christine. He knew she was sincere about his finally finding himself. Those punishing years of thinking she hated him for taking her love for granted were over.

Their meeting had revealed as much. He had seen it in her eyes and heard it in her voice: she understood he had been, simply, a mixed up kid. Will felt Christine's acceptance of him - *for that time in his life*, but a murder charge was a different story.

Will guessed fate intervened so that they could meet again, and was glad of it. He had wondered where she was, how much she or the ring of her laughter had changed.

They had always laughed together, often at something silly he said or a corny joke she told him. Christine had made Will feel like a king, which is why he called her his princess.

In one way or another, Kennedy had always loved Christine and now knew she felt the same way about him. He felt that magnets deep within their bodies drew them together.

Is there another woman like her on the face of the earth? he wondered. Only the jail stood in his way of knowing.

CHAPTER THIRTY

Mars Starr reveled in the rich dark soil beneath his feet. He carefully padded between the rows of climbing beans and butternut squash to the front of his garden – a mere stone's throw from the doorway to his cabin. There, the huge sunflowers followed the sun's arc with their big brown faces and bright yellow bonnets.

During the early spring, Mars had planted seeds of white sage across from them, where the soil was sandier. The plants had flourished in the summer sun, and he gathered them up a few weeks earlier, bound their stems together with string, and hung them to dry.

Starr examined the curled and browning leaves and sniffed at the bouquet. Its enhanced and aromatic intensity offset a loss in vibrancy. The sage was ready for smudging, and its smoke bath would cleanse him, Tonto, and their land of the depraved energy that had seeped into their lives over the past few months.

Three times in July and twice in August, Mars donned his diving gear to pull dead kids from the lakes up north and in the western part of the state, while their grieving families wept and watched from shore.

The temperature had soared close to a hundred one afternoon when detectives received a tip and sent Mars and Tonto on a search for a four year old who had been missing a week or more.

Tonto got a hit on the site. They discovered the child's mutilated body stuffed in the incinerator of an abandoned building near Raynham. For the first time, Mars vomited on the job.

A few days later, he and Tonto had found near the main drag in Brockton the body of a demented old man who had wandered from a nursing home and into the woods. He had tumbled into a gully and died there, naked, alone, and face down, in a pile of wet leaves - a fractured bone jutting out his grotesquely twisted leg.

Tomorrow morning, he and Tonto would meet Gillan and Ronan and search Freddy Nunn's property again, this time systematically - inside and out.

Mars was certain that the smudging's smoke bath would restore balance and clarity to their life's purpose and to that of his carving site and the block of cedar that stood ready for carving.

The sage crumpled easily between his fingers and fell softly into an abalone shell. When he struck a match, the sage flashed into bright flames then sizzled, smoldered, and glowed. The pungent scented smoke streamed into the air and around the site where the cedar stood.

Mars fanned the embers and cautiously combed the smoke with a hawk's feather, untangling the good energy from the bad, bad energy that could block his ritual. He encircled his land like the powerful engine of a train - dark smoke puffing and pouring from the abalone shell - as he rolled on along through his cabin, around his jeep, and under fruit trees.

As he passed the garden, Starr stopped briefly at his carving site. The smoke fanned out and drifted in languid ribbons around the cedar block. He traveled to his water barrel and wheelbarrow, and chugged across the yard to the shed where he fanned his ax, shovel, hoe, and rake.

Starr journeyed from the sun and into shade where he sighed, stopped, and knelt on the ground where his dog lay, curled and snoring. He lightly fanned the pungent smoke over and around him. Tonto lifted his head, sniffed the air, eyed his handler, and fell to sleep.

The ritual was complete.

He set out his carving tools and picked up the largest chisel. The night before, Mars had stripped the bark from the cedar and now contemplated the blank form that stood before him, reverently waiting for its spirit to speak to him.

That moment arrived. Mars gave thanks and touched the chisel to the cedar, marking a position for her eyes and nose and the height and width of her face. With closed eyes, he ran his long fingers over the block, gently feeling for each knot, protrusion, and depression in the wood that could become one with her face.

Later, when the carving was complete, Mars would set her form in stone. She would face south and watch over the summer garden that would bring bountiful gifts to his table. He picked up the chisel and slid it into the cedar's tissue. The nose took shape, straight, honest, and beautiful - like the base of the cedar tree that bore her.

Adoette would embody her name.

CHAPTER THIRTY ONE

Freddy Nunn sneered and swore at the words on his laptop. "What a bitch!" His fingers hovered over the keyboard until he hit the reply key and furiously typed.

"Dear Ms. Heartstone, I can't believe you found my real mother. Seeing that I can't come out to Michigan to meet up with you, and you can't give me the name over the Internet, I'll have to wait for the registered letter from you to find out who she is. Send it as soon as you can or let me know the day you go to the post office, so I can wait for the mailman; Sincerely, Frederick W. Nunn."

After sending the email, Nunn called the bank. "I'm still sick. The doctor says I'll be out for a week. I know, I know. You'll get your doctor's note! Yes, I know about Alfred Locke. And no, I'm not giving any money for flowers."

He slammed the phone, fell into his favorite chair, and sat in his dusky living room stroking his cat's silky ears. "I know, I know what you're thinking Paradise: We're going to have such a wonderful life. We're finally going to meet Mother."

Closing his eyes, Nunn smiled. "Life will be good again."

The chime of the doorbell clashed with Freddy's thoughts. "Who the hell is that?" he huffed, shooing Paradise to the floor. Nunn pulled back the curtain to peek out the window and saw police cars filling the driveway.

Ronan caught the movement of the curtain and stared at him, and Freddy broke into a sweat. The doorbell rang again.

Nunn straightened himself and stomped to the door. "Well, well, if it isn't the swaggering Sweede and his squadron of super sleuths. What the hell do you want?"

Sweede dangled a search warrant in his face. Startled, Freddy demanded, "Get that thing away from me!"

"Read it and weep Freddy. Now get the hell out of our way."

Freddy grabbed the search warrant and tore it to pieces. "That's what I think of your search warrant, Sherlock. Now get out!"

Sweede shoved him aside, and Gillan and Mars rushed into the hallway with Ronan and Tonto. Ted joined Sweede, and the detectives raced throughout the house searching everything in sight.

Mars and Gillan found the cellar, and the dogs feverishly sniffed, scampered, and zipped upstairs with their handlers in tow. They dashed to the second floor followed by the third, frantically sniffing in and around beds, bureaus, chairs, closets, piles of clothes, broken coat hangers, books, empty soda cans, paper plates, and stacks of magazines and mail.

Next, they sped to the attic.

"Don't you dare touch anything in my war room! And keep your dirty paws off my collectibles," Nunn howled, "or I'll sue you and your dogs! And I'm allergic to dog hair! You better hope I don't wind up in the emergency room with an asthma attack, or I'll call my lawyer! You're screwing-up my aura!"

Sweede rushed down the stairs, slammed into Freddy, elbowed his right kidney, and shoved him against the wall. "Shut the fuck up Freddy. Let us do our job!"

Nunn spit at Sweede, and the cops grabbed him. "You better let go of me or I'll report you to the authorities!" he shrieked.

Freddy wrenched and squirmed as the cops tightened their grip. "Let go of me! You're nothing but bullies, how do you sleep at night you boobs!" Tears streamed down his face. "I think I'm going to throw up. Take me to the bathroom, or I'll puke all over you!"

The officers dragged him to the kitchen and forced his face into a sink full of dishes. "If you're going to puke, puke in there where we can keep an eye on you - or you can knock it off and shut the fuck up!"

"I was only kidding," he rasped. "I wouldn't puke on you - I'd puke on your mother!"

The cop tightened his twist on Freddy's arm and jammed it farther against his back. "Then you're staying where you are, dick-head!"

Mars and Gillan hustled downstairs. "Sweede, there's nothing here. The dogs came up with zilch."

"Move outside and check the yard again."

Freddy wrung his face from the sink and caught sight of Sweede. "You've ruined my karma you bastard. You'll get yours!"

CHAPTER THIRTY TWO

Mickey Mercer fumbled with the keys to Will Kennedy's house, opened the door, stepped inside, and glanced at his watch. "Christine, you get the paperwork from the desk upstairs in the study. I'm going to take some pictures of where the bloody saw was found, then go down to the pond where they pulled out her cell and pocketbook. We've got about forty-five minutes. I've got to be in court by one."

"It's chilly in here," she said while buttoning her red blazer. "I never feel comfortable in another person's home unless they're here. It's too quiet, and I feel like a voyeur peeking into their lives."

Christine scanned the living room and shivered at the starkness of it: beige walls, no incidental or meaningful accents of furniture. No photographs of people with smiling faces, no plants, paintings, books, or easy chairs in close proximity, probably no comforting fire for two had ever blazed in the fireplace.

She peered into the kitchen and added, "It doesn't feel very homey in here."

"It wasn't much of a home." Mercer responded. "You know what they say, and my wife says it all the time: a house isn't a home without happiness. And from what Kennedy told Sudanski, love never lived here. It was just a place to hang their hats and sleep."

He held up the camera, peered through the viewer, shot, and headed to the rear of the house.

Will's study sharply contrasted to the bleakness Christine sensed in the rest of the house. Wide pine floorboards gleamed in the late morning sun and accented a handsome bookcase that lined the walls on both sides of the fireplace.

Christine recalled Will's love of boats and ships, thinking his yearning for the ocean had not changed. A few close-ups of him with head capped and nose clipped in a swimming relay hung near the fireplace. A grand painting of the sloop, *Jupiter,* hung above the mantle.

Snapshots of Will and his running buddies - arms slung over sweaty shoulders, holding medals in Olympic fashion - hung near prints of Bob 'Bullet' Hayes in the Tokyo Games of 1964. A lone photo of chess champ, Bobby Fisher, his head bowed in concentration, sat on Will's desk, a sleek, honey-colored, Danish design that felt smooth and sturdy under the palm of her hand.

She slid open the bottom draw and found the insurance papers, along with a few photos of Will and Judy, and Judy and some other guy. The width of Will's lapels and tie and Judy's hair-style were a giveaway - the pictures must have been taken in the late '60s or early '70s.

Running her fingertip over his face, Christine noted how young he looked, so rugged, and handsome and grinned with a bitter sweetness at the shyness of his smile.

"Will," she murmured, "I would never have figured you to marry a redhead with glasses and a space between her teeth, and she's wearing too much jewelry. You both look so happy. I'm glad you had some good times together."

Suddenly feeling a stifling sense of loss and isolation stir within her, she wearily left the room for the kitchen downstairs, where Mercer was waiting.

"How much was she worth?"

"Fifty thousand."

"Hmm, not much of a reason to murder her. He made a decent living, not much of a swinger, no girlfriends, and no debt. The DA is going to have a hard time figuring out a motive. I've got everything I need here and have to get to court. Are you going to interview Freddy Nunn?"

"Yes, and I read his deposition this morning."

"Be prepared, Christine. I hear he's a real weirdo."

"He won't be the first weirdo I've met - especially in this business."

CHAPTER THIRTY THREE

"Now, who the hell is this?" Infuriated, Freddy Nunn stomped to the door and flung it open. "What the hell do you want?" he demanded.

Christine flinched in astonishment. "Oh, Mr. Nunn, I didn't mean to disturb you. Should I come back at a more convenient time?"

"Um, no. Are you selling cosmetics? Because your makeup looks very nice."

"No, I'm a lawyer. May I come in?"

His body stiffened. "Are you part of Sweede's crew?" he asked suspiciously. "Because if you are, you can just leave or I'll throw you out like I threw him and his band of boobs out a few minutes ago!"

"My name is Christine O'Malley, and I represent Mr. William Kennedy, Judy's husband. He's been arrested for her murder."

Freddy smiled broadly. "Hurray, and I know all about it, you silly girl. Now, what do you want?"

"If you're willing, I'd like to discuss the initial statement you gave to Detectives Swenson and Smith about Judy Kennedy. It's nothing crucial, just a couple of points that need clarification."

"Are you crazy? Do you know how busy I am? Today is one of the most important days of my life! And I'm always being bothered by people like you - ruining it for me!" he complained waving a fat finger in her face. Christine stepped back.

"And don't try to wiggle out of it!"

"Mr. Nunn, I don't mean to upset you, I was hoping..."

"Hoping for what? To get Will off? Forget it. You're not getting anything from me," he screamed. "I said what I had to say to Ted and that swaggering Sweede.

"Do you know that Judy, my muse, my angel, spent over a year helping to find my birth mother? Did you know that? And wouldn't you know it, now that she's dead, my mother has been found. And I owe it all to Judy," he sobbed, "and I have a terrible headache."

"I'm so sorry to hear that," she stammered. "Can I get you a couple of aspirins, or open a window? It's a little stuffy in here." He ignored her.

"Mr. Nunn, I'm so sorry for your loss, but it must be of some comfort to know that Judy was such a great help to you. The friendship you shared revealed a great gift. You've found your birth mother. It must have been a very special moment in your life."

Freddy wrinkled his nose, as he turned his fleshy face to hers. "Are you stupid? You must be, because *my moment* doesn't matter as much, if Judy isn't here to share it with me."

He planted his hands on his hips and looked her up and down. "And anyways, I wouldn't expect a lawyer like you to understand what I'm going through, because you obviously have no heart!"

His voice rose to a feverish pitch. "You lawyers are all the same! It's all about money - money, money, money, twisting words around and preying on people like me. And there's so much malice around me," he shrieked, "and so much ugliness, that it's making me sick! And you're making it worse! It's all evil! And if you don't leave me alone, my head is going to blow up! Now get out! Go play in traffic, Sweetie!"

CHAPTER THIRTY FOUR

Christine pulled into a parking spot near the end of Carson beach, unwrapped her sandwich, and sat leisurely sipping her tea. "Freddy Nunn," she uttered, "you are a major weirdo." She put the window down and leaned her head on the seat rest. The sun felt good on her face, and a cool breeze flowed through her hair and softly brushed her lashes. She soon drifted to sleep and dreamed about Freddy Nunn.

Dressed as a dentist, Christine chided him. "Come on. Come on," she said, waving a hammer and roll of tape. "Let's fix those teeth."

"No, no!" Freddy screamed in terror.

"Have it your way, sonny, but let's take some pictures of those choppers and get the ball rolling."

"I'll take my own pictures!" he cried. "Here, look at this. Here's one of my cat. Can you fix his teeth first?"

"I've never seen a red cat!" she said laughing.

Freddy anxiously shuffled through his pictures. "Here's another one of Will. It's not very good because he's crying. He's always crying."

A child's sobbing awoke Christine. A young mother knelt on the beach, meticulously brushing sand from her toddler's hands and knees, then tenderly wiped his tears and kissed his cheek.

Christine watched them stroll away, hand in hand. She yawned, stretched, and pondered her dream before wrapping her sandwich and driving to the office so that Mercer could look at the photographs of Will, Judy, and Freddy.

Mercer hastily closed a golf digest and flipped it over. "How did things go, Christine?"

"It didn't, at least not in the way I hoped it would. Freddy wouldn't give me any information and practically threw me out of the house. He said that Sweede and his gang were there earlier today and that he had thrown them out."

"I wonder what the DA was looking for. I'm going to put in a few calls."

He punched in the numbers and blathered, "Hey, Pete, its Mickey Mercer. How about those Red Sox? Nope, they should trade him. He's a bum, we need batters!"

With the photos in hand, Christine returned a few minutes later, but Mercer was still on the phone.

"Are you sure about that? Okay. Thanks a lot, I owe you one." He hung up, clasped his hands behind his head, and leisurely leaned into his chair.

"Christine, Gillan and Mars Starr were at Freddy Nunn's the other day. They went back there today with Sweede and his boys. Did Gillan mention anything to you about it?"

"I haven't seen or talked to Gillan in quite a while."

"Did Freddy Nunn tell you what they were looking for?"

"I told you, Mercer, Freddy Nunn hates lawyers, and he practically threw me out!"

"I just want to be sure." Checking his watch, he stood and stretched his stringy arms. "Well, it's cocktail time, and I could use a sandwich. Let's go."

"I just ate."

"Well I haven't."

"Mercer, I want you to take a look at these photos."

"I'll look at them over dinner. I want to get to the restaurant before it gets too crowded."

"You may want to call and make reservations."

•••

Court adjourned for the day, and the waterfront restaurant across from Hanover Street was bustling with activity. Roberto adjusted his bow tie and floated by the waiting lawyers, white collar criminals, politicians and cops.

"Ah, Mr. Mercer, it is good that you made reservations."

Roberto turned and bowed to Christine. Regally lifting her hand, he said, "I will take Attorney Christine."

Mercer shuffled along behind them.

Roberto protectively maneuvered her through the crowded dining room and drew a chair. "Are you comfortable, Miss Christine?"

She nodded and smiled at him. "Oh, yes. Thank you, Roberto. I've had quite a day. I'm glad to be here, and you're one in a million. I'm in heaven."

"If you feel that you are in heaven, Miss Christine, it is because you are an angel!"

He nodded hastily to someone in the wings and snapped his fingers. "Jorge, see to Miss Christine at once."

Mickey Mercer faced a window and squinted at the sun's glare, swearing and muttering he tried to avoid it by shifting sideways. It did not help.

As he watched Mercer struggling to move his chair, Roberto snickered and turned his back, lifted a pencil, and leisurely checked the reservations list.

"You don't look very happy, Christine. Don't worry about not getting a statement from Freddy Nunn. We're all set."

"It's not that. There's something else. I mean, I know he's not playing with a full deck. He's practically living in squalor, and I do feel so sorry for him, but his reactions are so over the top. In a matter of thirty seconds," she said, counting on her fingers, "he cried, laughed, pouted, screamed, and accused me of something like ruining his 'special moment.'

"He claimed Judy Kennedy helped him find his biological mother. He got the news today. He's waiting to find out her name. Then Sweede and his boys showed up and searched his house. And I was on their heels. He ordered me out of the house and told me to go play in traffic!"

Mercer looked from the menu, laughing. "I told you he's crazy!"

She leaned the palm of her hand against her chin. "It's more than that."

Mercer slurped his drink and smacked his lips. "They make a great Southern Comfort Old Fashioned here."

"Didn't your parents teach you anything about table manners? Didn't you learn anything in law school, like the finer points of communication - like listening?"

"Nope," he said glancing at the menu. "Have you ever tried the gazpacho here?"

"Mercer, I'd like to discuss Freddy Nunn. He worked at the bank. He may know more than he's telling anyone."

Swirling the ice cubes in his glass, Mercer sat in thought but his face revealed a cynical smirk. "Christine, Freddy Nunn doesn't have the brains or the guts to kill a fly or fly a kite. I heard that he's got the IQ of a tomato. He couldn't sneak into Texas with a map, a compass, and a GPS.

"And, he's a pathological liar. People like him are usually afraid to lie to authority figures on anything important. They lie about silly shit to make themselves feel worthy.

"Will Kennedy is a different story. He's got the history and a rap sheet to back it up. You don't believe Will's innocent act is fake? You don't believe he's a liar?"

A burning flush rose in her face. "I don't know. I've never thought of Will as a liar or someone with murder in his blood. I mean, he was a sensitive and gentle soul. I interviewed him the other day, and I don't think he's changed!"

Mercer groaned. "Christine, gentle people don't hold innocent people up at gun point or bash them over the head and sever their ears with broken beer bottles. Guys like Kennedy remember every little slight or injustice ever done to them. They carry it around for years and then they just blow!"

Christine studied Mercer, as he fidgeted with his straw.

"You know what, Mercer? I've got a few really good books on psychological profiling. You can borrow them anytime you want. Your analysis is so twisted and so absurd that it's almost pitiful!"

"You're the one that's absurd and pitiful! And you know what else? You're in the wrong profession! You should be a social worker or sitting in some loft writing romance novels.

You know the type I mean - good girl loves bad boy, bad boy sees the light, settles down with good girl, have good kids, and they all live happily ever after."

He speared the bright red cherry from his drink and popped it into his mouth.

Christine's dark eyes blazed. "Will Kennedy never touched me. We dated when I was fifteen years old. He was a bad-boy, but I didn't care. I loved everything about him.

"I think I saw clear into his soul, his vulnerability, his goodness, his confusion. I didn't understand what I was feeling, but now I do. We were soul mates.

"Will Kennedy has core goodness. I don't think he killed his wife!"

Mercer sneered. "Teenagers run on feelings. Do you think it would be the same way now? Come on, Christine, grow up! And, if you think I missed Listening 101 in law school, than you must have missed Feelings Aren't Facts 101.

"Just because you feel something, doesn't mean it's true. Feelings aren't facts, especially for females like you who need to recuse themselves because they were in love with the guy they're defending for the murder of his wife!"

Her voice escalated in frustration. "Look at how he lives his life for crying out loud! He sponsors paraplegics for Veteran's Day fishing trips. He donates thousands to Pauling Rehab. He's a swimming teacher, and he and his crew clean a safe house for victims of domestic violence for nothing, every damn week. Those are the facts!

"And as far as his wife was concerned, she had some type of personality disorder. She was a pathological liar with mental illness! And we'll get her doctor to testify to that! Will felt sorry for her and put up with her antics for years!"

Mercer shook his head. "That's only his side of the story. What about the evidence Christine. Huh, what about it? Will Kennedy is going to stay where he belongs - in jail. I don't care what you or Charlie think - we'll never get him off. He's a murderer and the DA has the evidence to prove it!"

"Does Charlie know how you feel?"

Mercer drained his drink. "Screw him. Are you ready for another drink?"

"No, I'm not, and there's something else I need to talk about."

"Christine, don't tell me you're pregnant with Kennedy's kid?"

"What's your point? We're sitting here discussing a case, and you're making crude, sexist comments. You sound like a sixteen-year-old in the boys' locker room."

"Come on. Come on, Christine. I'm only kidding."

"Well, I'm not! Why don't you grow up? I'm trying to explain to you that, as part of Will's defense team, we…"

Mercer's faded blue eyes moved beyond her. "Hey, look who's here. It's Gillan and Sweede," he said, waving them to their table.

Christine shook her head. "Lucky you, Mercer. Saved by the bell!"

Sweede smiled cordially at the two attorneys. "What's this, double trouble?"

"It could be, but we're stuck with Will Kennedy, the lame duck! What's up, Sweede?"

"Not much, busy day, you know, the usual stuff." He turned from Mercer and motioned to the waiter. "Set us up."

Gillan broke in. "Jorge forget my usual. Bring me a scotch on the rocks with a soda chaser. And, an antipasto for four with extra anchovies."

Christine threw her head back and laughed. "I'll say you guys had a busy day!"

Gillan bit into a piece of bread and nodded. "You said it. How are you doing, Christine?"

"I'm doing…" Mercer interrupted. "She's doing fine, Gillan. I heard you searched Freddy Nunn's house today."

Christine frowned.

"Boy, news travels fast. How did you find out we were at Nunn's?"

"I've got my contacts. You brought your dogs up there and found blood!"

"You've got your days wrong, Mercer. I found some evidence a while ago and went back with Mars. I got a search warrant and we went back today with Sweede. We didn't find anything. The results of the DNA from what me and Mars found won't be in for weeks."

With his pencil poised, Jorge asked for the investigators' orders.

Christine sipped her wine. "Gillan, I'm curious about what sent you up there in the first place?"

"It was kind of a crazy thing, sort of a weird coincidence. I didn't know it, but Freddy Nunn lives about a quarter of a mile from me. A couple of weeks ago, Ronan picked up a gunpowder scent, and we followed it up to Nunn's place. I found a button and a shell casing and called in Mars Starr.

"He and Tonto picked up some blood, tissue, and hair from a shallow depression and a little more from a drag track on the far side of the yard. And they picked up a nose clip from under some bushes."

Mercer rubbed his nose. "What the hell's a nose clip? Do you mean like a pierced earring?"

"No. Swimmers wear them so water does doesn't get up and into their nose and screw up their sinuses."

"I've never heard of anything like that," Mercer admitted.

Sweede scoffed. "Where the hell did you grow up, in a desert?"

"No, I grew up in Attleboro."

"It figures – just about the same thing."

Christine nudged him. "Oh, come on, Sweede. Gillan, tell us, any speculation about the items from Freddy's yard?"

He pointed to Sweede. "You'll have to ask this guy."

Sweede yawned and rubbed his eyes. "The only thing we know for sure is that Freddy works at the bank with Alfred Locke, who, by the way, doesn't live far from him. A million and a half dollars is missing, as is Ginger Stoolman. Judy Kennedy is dead. A shell casing, button, bloody tissue, and nose clip were found in Nunn's yard.

"Kennedy and Locke swim regularly and both use nose clips as do most people who live ocean side or have a pool. Nunn's neighborhood is full of them."

Christine arched her brows. "So, it's actually two different cases."

"That's right, the missing money could be the catalyst and biggest motive for murder, and the one that will pile on what we already have on Kennedy, who was friendly with Locke. We're just connecting dots.

"Kennedy is a smart guy with a rap sheet. It's hard to believe that he didn't know what his wife was doing. You're going to have a hard time proving his innocence. And that's that!" he laughed before motioning to Gillan.

"I'm starved, pass me the antipasto."

As Christine poked a bit of bright green lettuce with her fork, Mercer watched, snickered, leaned backwards, and laced his fingers behind his head.

"What's wrong Attorney O'Malley? Feeling defeated? Did Sweede dampen your appetite? Are you afraid the truth is too hard to swallow or does it make you sick to your stomach?"

Suppressing the tears welling in her eyes, Christine laid down her fork on the white tablecloth, slowly and deliberately lifted a napkin, and wiped her mouth. Turning to the detectives, she said, "You'll pardon my colleague's apathy."

"Mercer, your remarks reflect a gross lack of insight into human behavior. And, I remind you of the words spoken by Robert Frost, the esteemed American poet: 'The jury consists of twelve persons chosen to decide who has the *best* lawyer.'"

After a sip of ice water, Christine cut into her steak.

A scarlet glow crossed Mercer's face, and the detectives quickly looked away. He drained his glass and faced Sweede and Gillan. "She knows Will Kennedy. They used to date! And she needs to recuse herself or the judge will do it for her. He won't like it, no matter how long ago it was."

"Love is a wonderful thing, Mercer, especially when you're fifteen. And I can speak for myself," said Christine.

She turned from Mercer to the investigators. "I was at Will Kennedy's today, going over insurance papers, and found some old photographs of him and Judy and more recent ones of Judy and Freddy," she said, shuffling through her attaché. She pulled out the photos and methodically laid them side by side. "Anything look familiar?"

When Sweede gathered the photographs, held them to the dim light, and squinted, Christine handed him her glasses.

"Wow, are these prescription?"

"Yes, but don't look at me while you're wearing them. I don't want to panic you into not paying for my dinner."

Sweede studied the pictures and shrugged. "I don't see anything."

At his turn, Gillan added, "Sorry, Christine, nothing jumps out at me except for the gaps in their teeth. The neighbors on either side of my house and the guy across the street all have an opening between their front teeth that I could drive my Harley through. They all need braces!"

Gillan passed the pictures to Mercer, who ignored and flipped them to Christine, saying only, "So what?"

CHAPTER THIRTY FIVE

N unn heard the postal truck's familiar groan as it climbed the hill and jerked to a screechy halt. Fanning himself with a magazine, he raced to the window. Dean jumped from the truck, adjusted a bulging pouch hanging from his shoulder, and hastily walked in the opposite direction.

Freddy raced to the door and screamed, "Hey! Do you have a registered letter for me?"

Dean hesitated, spun around, and trudged up the walkway. "I haven't got anything for you to sign, but I'm keeping an eye open for you."

"You need to keep both eyes open."

"If you have a letter coming that needs a signature, you bet I'll bring it to you. I've been delivering mail here for eight years!"

With tears welling in his eyes, Freddy replied, "Dean, I told you how important that letter is to me! You know how long I've been waiting. I need to know who my mother is."

"And like I told you, I was adopted too. My mother found me, and we hooked up, everything is cool. It'll be cool for you, too. But, for the umpteenth time, as soon as the post office gets the letter, you'll get the letter; trust me, okay?"

Freddy sniffled and blew his nose. "Okay, Dean. By the way, can I buy some pot?"

"No can do, Buddy. My brother got busted. But you can buy some cookies," he said, motioning to two approaching figures. "Your neighbors are here selling them. The whole neighborhood is selling them. I've bought eight boxes so far this morning!"

Grace Lafontaine clutched hold of her daughter's hand and cautiously waddled up the walkway. She was pregnant again, her feet and ankles had swelled like balloons under the immense weight of her inflated belly, and her time was near. "What a beautiful morning we're blessed with," she said, squinting at the bright blue sky.

"It sure is," said Dean. "No clouds in sight, but you look as if you're ready to go any minute. How are you, Mrs. LaFontaine?"

"You're so very kind to ask. I'm well, well indeed," she said, gently patting her belly. "In another week or so, Michael Vincent will be with us."

"Yes," said Faith eagerly. "Michael is on his way. I'm going to have a new brother!"

"Well, Faith, while you're waiting for him, I've got some mail for your Dad."

"Thank you so much, Dean," said Grace. "The reverend is working in his office this morning. Would you mind rapping on the door and let him know that his mail is here? He's waiting for his monthly directives. Faith is here selling Cookies for Kid's Camp through our church."

Dean smiled at Faith. "I'll sign up for a box, and Mr. Nunn will, too," he said handing him the order sheet. "Freddy, get the double chocolate, they're pretty good."

Faith handed him a pencil. "Thank you. We're having a contest. The church that sells the most cookies wins free passes to Spooky World."

Grace lovingly stroked her daughter's long blonde ponytail. "Faith puts so much effort into everything she does."

Freddy's eyes filled with tears. "That's so wonderful to know."

"Yes, it is. Faith has been a joy to everyone who knows her since the day she was born."

He burst into tears. "Faith, you're so lucky," he sobbed. "I hope my real mother loves me like your mother loves you."

Dean rolled his eyes. "Well, got to get moving. Have a good one."

Grace offered a tissue, but Freddy waved her off.

"I have one," he bawled. "Mrs. Lafontaine, did you know that I'm adopted? I'm waiting for a letter that tells me who my real mother is!"

"Oh Freddy," she said laying a hand on her heart. "I had no idea! The reverend and I thought Mrs. Nunn was your biological mother. You look exactly like her - red hair and all! She was so genteel, so lovely, and you two were devoted to each other. We all miss her. And now, here you are hoping to meet your real mother. We pray she'll be just as lovely."

Faith nodded. "You'll find out pretty soon, Mr. Nunn. And then everything will be all right."

Grace gently placed her hand on Faith's slender shoulders.

"Faith and I would like to pray with you, Freddy."

"But I'm a Budslam!"

"A Divine Creator loves all souls – regardless of how we refer to it or worship. If our intentions are good and true, our prayers are heard. Things may not turn out exactly as we expect, but goodness comes from it."

Freddy sucked in his stomach, squared his shoulders, and squeezed his eyes shut. "All right I'm ready. Go ahead."

"May I lead, Mommy?"

"Certainly."

Faith extended her willowy arms. "Let's all join hands."

"I'm not holding hands," he muttered, "too many germs."

"Faith, some people aren't used to holding hands. We'll just bow our heads."

"Okay, Mommy, can I begin now?"

"Yes dear, you can begin now."

She firmly pressed her palms together. "Dear Jesus," she said boldly, "please help Mr. Nunn get his letter soon, so he'll know who his mother is. He's so sad. We know that he'll be happy when he meets her, and then we'll all be happy for him. Thank you, Jesus. Amen."

CHAPTER THIRTY SIX

Christine sat in her pew, reflecting on the wooden crucifix that hung on gilded chains above the altar. Flickering candlelight cast a radiant glow on those worshipers kneeling there: heads bowed, hands clasped, and lips moving in silent prayers.

She felt a greater sense of peace in the empty church where it was quiet and without interruption, spoken words, collective refrains, or required responses. She knew those actions instilled in her a sense of sanctity, whether praying alone or watching in wonder as the sunlight streamed through the stained glass windows. Brilliant blues, glowing greens, and fiery reds cast their colorful reflections around the great nave, like so many scattered and broken rainbows.

Christine closed her eyes and inhaled the scent of warm candle wax and the pungent fragrance of burning incense. Her thoughts became quiet and still - conscious only of the breaths that passed life through her being. She knelt and bowed her head.

"Dear Lord, you know why I'm here," she murmured. "I don't know why you brought me to this place and this time, to Will, after so many years. I thought you'd let me catch my breath and recover a bit after all I've been through since Jeffrey's death and the mess he left me in. But you have other plans. And I know that I'm exactly where I should be in my life. I trust you."

She shifted in her seat. "You know I can't defend Will. I'm not sure how to help him or what I'm doing here. I think he's innocent, but there's so much evidence stacked against him. And I made a fool out of myself with those photographs. You're the only one who knows the truth. I need clear direction from *you*. My gut instincts aren't working so well right now. And I don't want to stand in my own shadow any more. I've fooled myself for long enough with Jeffrey. Mercer may have been right about my being naive."

Christine wiped the tears from her eyes. "So, I'll just mark time, do what I can do, and wait for your direction. In the meantime, please bring the right people and circumstances to Will's defense - if he's innocent. I ask this in the name of your son, Jesus Christ. Amen."

The quick steps of her heels echoed over the marble tiled floor, as she passed the long rows of mahogany pews and the saintly statues clothed in flowing robes - reminders of Christians who had triumphed in their faith, they stood eternally vigilant in their Lord's house.

She stopped, blessed herself, pushed open a heavy wooden door, stepped into the sparkling sunshine, wiped tears from her eyes, and went for a long walk; later she intended to call Charlie Sudanski.

After spending the afternoon in district court, she stopped for an early dinner before going home and rested comfortably with her feet up, watching the news.

Sudanski called. "How was your day?"

"Hi Charlie. Things are going all right. I got a continuance for Kim Gallahue, and Aileen Duffy is officially divorced. I got her a really good deal. And the zoning board is contesting the proposed expansion of Banuk's trailer park. How was the wedding?"

"The wedding was great. Pamela looked like a princess, and Marie took a lot of pictures. They'll be on her site later today. We'll be home in a few days."

"I can't wait to see them, and can't wait for you to get back. Charlie, I need to talk to you about Will. I dated him in my teens."

"I know, Christine, Mercer already called me. I spoke with Will and told him you had to recuse yourself and why. We have enough information to work with for now. I'll be home on Thursday and pick it up from there. I offered to send my brother, but Will refused. He said he'd sit tight until I got back. Alice and Mercer can take care of any paperwork."

"Charlie, I'll be doing some background work for Will, some research, some digging around."

"Christine, stay put for now. Work on Paul O'Connell's case. He's innocent, and we're going to prove it! I'm going to let Mercer go when I get back. He's the type that will spill his guts and try to have you disbarred for working on Will's behalf in any way, shape, or form, okay?"

"Okay, Charlie, I'll work on the O'Connell case."

She turned on the light, the television off, and opened a copy of Dunn's *Conversations in Paint*. The clock's intrusive ticking marked the rhythm of moments passing, like the heartbeat of every living creature. With each second, rain or shine, sun or moon, day after day, its brass pendulum swung relentlessly, as her thoughts turned to Will in that bleak and miserable jail.

The deep, gilded glow of a nearly full moon shone bright and beautiful in the night sky and beckoned to her. She rose and moved to the window. Venus, the glittering showgirl, dangled a whisper away from the night's golden orb.

"I hope Will can see you, Venus. I hope you're showing off for him. Remind him that life can sparkle and shine again."

CHAPTER THIRTY
SEVEN

G race Lafontaine winced at the sound of the doorbell. Exhausted and bloated, she gathered her crochet hooks and yarn and struggled from her rocking chair.

"I'll get it, Mommy. I hope it's the cookies. It is!" Faith cried as she peered through the window and eagerly waved to the deliveryman. "I'll get the order sheets. Daddy will help sort them out."

Grace gratefully leaned into the rocking chair, gently rubbing her swollen hands over her inflated belly.

Her husband, Reverend Lafontaine, finished writing his Sunday sermon, locked his cramped office, and joined Grace in their comfortably littered study. She looked flushed and bloated. "How are you feeling?"

"Are you finished with your sermon, Lawrence?"

"Yes, I'm sorry it took so long."

"Faith's cookies have arrived."

"I know. She and I are going to sort them out. You relax. I think our Michael is going to arrive sooner than later."

"I think you're right, Lawrence, I need to practice my breathing."

"We both need to practice your breathing. I'm sorry I've been so busy lately."

She gently rubbed his shoulder. "We're blessed with the progress the church has made. You've made such a difference in everyone's life. Lawrence, you've been deliberate in the Word, and so inspiring. The parishioners are so pleased with your efforts."

He blushed. "The person who's inspiring is Mrs. Keith. She stopped by the office and dropped off a roast chicken dinner and that great gingerbread she makes every fall. Talk about inspired! I'm inspired to eat. Stay here. I'll set the table."

"Bless that woman's heart. I'll write her a note of thanks in the morning, but I'm not so hungry, Lawrence. I need to rest."

"Are you having labor pains?"

"No, I'm just tired. Here's our Faith with her order sheets."

Faith scrambled to her father's lap. "Daddy, I think I've got everything sorted out. It comes to thirty one boxes of cookies, and I matched each box to every person's name. But you'll have to check them," she said cheerfully. "Did you get your new glasses yet?"

"Not yet."

He glanced over the order sheets. "Good job, Faith. We'll deliver them tomorrow, and, when we're finished, we'll go to Friendly's and have hot fudge sundaes. We're going to have a busy afternoon. Have you shown your mother what Mrs. Keith brought her?"

"Do you mean the ginger bread?"

"No, the other things, the yellow and…"

"Oh, I know what you mean." Faith scampered to the kitchen and returned, carefully carrying a small blue vase. "Mommy, Mrs. Keith sent these to you. She said something like simple flowers are the best flowers. I don't know what she meant, but here are some daisies for you. Mrs. Keith said that they're the last of this summer's bloom, but still fresh and perky!"

CHAPTER THIRTY EIGHT

C hristine smoothed a blanket while looking up at her mother. "You look nice and comfortable."

Rose scowled, "Well, I'm not. And I don't know where these florists get their roses - probably from somewhere down south. They're not very healthy looking. The petals are all brown around the tips! Who wants yellow roses with brown tips? I don't! And I hate white mums. They remind me of funerals. Take them out of here! And who sent the pink arrangement? Christine, read the card to me."

"It's from the staff at Marsh House. They wish you a speedy recovery and invite you to tour again when you're feeling better. Mother, you really need to make a decision. You can't keep changing your mind," Christine said before handing the card to her mother.

"I can't read this! I don't have my glasses with me. And I don't like people pressuring me into a move that I don't want to make. They're just a bunch of phonies!" she said while yanking the sheet and flattening it. "And I wish people would stop sending plants and dish gardens. I've got enough plants. Natalie, take the one with the pink bow home with you."

While Christine fussed with the bouquets - pinching dead blooms, repositioning the flowers and pouring fresh water into the arrangements, Natalie and Phillip, sat sullenly on either side of Rose's hospital bed.

"Phillip, be a good son and adjust the head of my bed."

He toyed with the bed control. "Mother, would you like your head up or down?"

"Up, I need to go higher. No, that's too high; bring it down a bit, a little more." She fidgeted for a comfortable position. "Phillip this is almost perfect! Just bring it down a little lower. That's too much, Dear. I need to go back up."

Rose bounced her head on the pillow a few times, and finally settled back. "Good. That feels better. Now go and find the nurse and tell her I need another pillow. In fact get two. Tell her my elbow is sore. I think my tendonitis is acting up. I'll need to keep my arm elevated. And tell her I need my pain medication. Oh, and raise the head again - just a teeny, weeny bit."

Phillip handed her the bed control. "Mother, this blue button is for head up and this yellow button is for head down. You may be better at it than I am. I can't seem to get it right."

"Oh no, Dear, I can't use that control. My left arm is so sore. And my fingers on both hands are stiff. I can barely bend them. Now go find the nurse."

Natalie smirked and watched Phillip wander from the room in search of a nurse.

Moments later, Dr. Sal Gaboni breezed through door. "Rose," he roared with a thunderous clap of his hands, "your daughters are chips off the old block. I've never seen two more beautiful girls than the Sandonato girls! They've got your genes, Rose. They've got your genes for sure! And they're smart - smart as whips!"

Drawing a quick breath, he continued, "I know you're as proud of them as Lena and I are of our Rita. Did you know that Rita is a podiatrist? She has a big practice in Manhattan, and she's a consultant for that morning medical show on Channel 9! Her husband, Anthony, is one of the top speech-writers for the head of the Republican National Committee, and his cousin married into the Nixon family!

"Rose, we're blessed!"

She picked at the sheets. "Dr. Gaboni, my elbow is so sore. I think my tendonitis is acting up again."

He quickly cupped her elbow in his hand. "All right, now, extend your arm." Dr. Gaboni firmly pressed against the boney knob on the outside of her elbow and then into the depression and soft tissue around it.

"*Ouch!*"

"Rose you've got a bit of tendonitis, nothing a good shot of cortisone won't help. I'll see you in my office for that. The good news is that you didn't have a heart attack, and your gall bladder is fine, just fine - probably just a case of indigestion. You know Rose, we are what we eat. I'll have the nurse go over a food list with you just to make sure you're not eating anything that causes too much gas!"

Natalie rolled her eyes and whispered to Christine, "He should know, he's got plenty of it."

Dr. Gaboni spun around pointing his finger. "What do you think, Christine? What do you think Natalie? Is Dr. Sal Gaboni wrong or is Dr. Sal Gaboni right?"

Natalie crossed her arms over her chest. "Oh, you're right, Dr. Gaboni. You are what you eat!"

Christine nodded. "Yes, you're right."

He twirled to Rose and bellowed, "You have to do what's best, and we're all in agreement: no fatty foods! And by the way, Rose, I heard you and the girls were touring over at Marsh House.

"I think the thought of moving is giving you the jitters, making you nervous and upset. It could be causing that indigestion.

"But I'm here to tell you that it's the best thing for you. My sister, Angie, moved in there about six months ago. She loves it. Lena and I go over there every Wednesday night and have dinner with her. It's only three dollars per guest!

"And Rose, I'm personally extending an invitation for you to join us for dinner every Wednesday night. Of course, you won't have to pay because you'll be living there! So plan on it, Rose. Plan on moving to Marsh House and having dinner with Dr. Sal Gaboni and his favorite gals every Wednesday night!"

He smoothed his vest, buttoned the jacket of his pin-striped suit, and beamed before her. "Rose, life is good!"

She tugged at the bed sheets. "Well if *you* think it's a good idea, I'll..."

"Of course it's a good idea!" he blasted. "It's the only way to go! Rose, I've been your doctor for almost fifty years. Would I steer you wrong?"

Natalie eyed him warily and whispered to her sister, "That blow hard owns Marsh House!"

"Shush. It makes Mom feel better."

Rose glowed and she gushed. "Well, Doctor, ah, Sal, it's settled! You've settled my nerves! I'm moving to Marsh House! Christine and Natalie were just going to my house to sort through some things. I feel better already. I feel better just knowing that I'll be having dinner with you, Angie, and Lena every Wednesday night."

He hastily patted her hand. "Of course, you feel better, Rose. Of course you do."

With the pillows stuffed in his arms, Phillip rambled to his mother's bedside while a weary-looking nurse trailed him.

Christine and Natalie made a hasty retreat.

•••

Natalie knelt by the cedar chest. "You know Christine, Dr. Gaboni is so full of himself. He neglected to mention that he and his holding company own Marsh House. And they want it filled to capacity by year's end."

"I know, but there's no conflict of interest that I'm aware of. He's not treating patients there. It's all right, Natalie. Mom's now willing to make the effort."

"Well, if you say so I guess we should begin where we left off." Natalie opened the cedar chest and handed the letter to her sister who smoothed it on her lap. "It's from Will Kennedy. He must have written it almost thirty years ago," Christine whispered.

After reading it, she wiped her eyes. Natalie watched her carefully fold and place the letter in its faded envelope. "What did it say?"

"He wrote it after he was released from jail. He apologized for the way he treated me. Will wanted to start over. Will had plans for a business - plans for us, and asked that I marry him. He wrote his new address and phone number here on the bottom. Oh Natalie, Will must have waited for me, but I never came. I never came, because I didn't know. Mom hid his letter from me."

"She wanted to protect you," Natalie said, gently rubbing her sister's back. "Christine, if Will Kennedy did murder his wife, maybe Ma protected you more than you know. And at the very least, you have closure."

"Yes, but Will doesn't."

"Maybe he doesn't need it!"

"Maybe he *does* need it! Natalie, we can finish this tomorrow night. I've got to get going."

"Where to?"

"I'm going to see Will. I need to show him this letter!"

"You can't. You have to recuse yourself!"

"The correctional officers don't know that!"

●●●

Christine stared at her hands and then the fluorescent lights in the waiting room of the jail. Her skin looked sallow beneath their glow.

Officer Mathew Dee rambled around the stark room, scooping scraps of paper from the floor and straightening chairs.

"Busy evening, Mattie?"

"You bet. The surveillance cameras were streaming away tonight. They sure help! Kennedy will be down in a minute."

Will entered and stopped abruptly. "Christine, what are you doing here? I'm surprised to see you. I mean, it's good to see you, but I don't want you to get in trouble. I know that you had to recuse…"

She silently warned him to stop. "There's something I want you to read," she said, handing the letter to him.

"What's this?" he asked before seating himself. After reading words written so long ago, Kennedy quietly wondered what to say next, afraid to say what he really felt.

Why didn't you answer me?

Will searched for the right words, found none, and decided to play it safe. Flashing a grin as bright as the noonday's sun, he said, "There's one good thing about this. I was sober when I wrote it!"

"That's you, Will, always looking on the bright side!"

After a second look at the letter, his grin faded like the dusk. "Christine, why show this to me now?"

"I just found it. Natalie and I were sorting through some things in my mother's cedar chest. Your letter was packed away there. My mother got it but never gave it to me. I went off to college thinking that you just didn't care or that you were angry with me. I tried to find you, but couldn't. I just wanted you to know that. It's important to me - you were that important to me." Tears clouded her eyes.

"Listen to me," she scoffed, "talking like a teenager."

Studying her face, Will swallowed hard before responding, "It works for me, Christine. It explains a lot. I thought *you* were mad at me for all these years, I thought you hated me, hated me for what I was and how I treated you."

She wiped away her tears. "I could never hate you, and I never doubted your worth. I've always believed in you."

"Thank you, Christine. What you're saying means a lot to me. Do you believe that I didn't murder my wife?"

She hesitated and thought about the evidence mounting against him and the nose clip sitting in forensics. "Yes, yes, I believe you. I just can't do much to help, but Charlie can."

"I know he can, and I'm counting on it," he said, glancing at the barred windows. "It's getting late. Thanks for coming, Christine."

As he watched her quickly walk away, Kennedy motioned to the waiting guard, who then hustled him to his cell.

Christine tucked away the letter, buttoned her sweater, and stepped into the cold, windy night and a deserted parking lot. While sheets of grey clouds streamed across the sky and hid the moon, a skunk ambled by and disappeared under the bushes.

The season was changing, and a chill hung in the air.

CHAPTER THIRTY NINE

Afternoon sunlight skimmed the tree tops and revealed dying green leaves turning to brilliant yellows and burning reds - autumn's attire for the maples and oaks that lined Freddy Nunn's street. He turned away from the window, popped a few peanuts into his mouth, and impatiently checked the time; Dean should have been here by now.

He leaned against his cluttered countertop, cupped greasy hands around his mouth, and bellowed, "Calling the US Postal Service, calling Dean, calling Dean.

"You should have been here by now. You postal poop hole, I want my letter. If you don't have it, I hope a sixteen-wheeler runs over your beagle!"

Nunn dragged a chair across the living room and stationed himself by the front window waiting for the mail while watching Reverend Lafontaine and Faith loading bright red boxes of cookies into their car.

"Oh, Dean," he bellowed, "our cookies are here!" Nunn shook the last of his peanuts onto the windowsill then crossed his fingers and made a wish. *Please, please, bring my letter.*

When the mail truck groaned to a halt, Freddy jumped from his chair and dashed to the door.

"Well, my fine, feathered friend," he hollered, "you're late. Do you have it? Do you have my letter?"

Dean hesitated at the sound of Nunn's voice, stopped, abruptly fished through his pouch for the letter, and hiked up the walk, huffing and red faced. "You bet your ass I do," he snarled through clenched teeth. "You ever talk like that to me again, and you'll be picking up your mail at the post office!"

"But, Dean, you know how long I've been waiting."

"I don't give two shits how long you've been waiting. You crossed the line. Sign here, you freakin' nut."

With shaking hands, Freddy grabbed the pen and scribbled his name before Dean thrust the letter at him and headed down the walkway.

"Hey, Dean," yelled Freddy, "I'm going to call the post office and tell them you sold me some pot!"

Dean hollered, "Have a nice day, Mr. Nunn," waved with his left hand, and gave him the finger with his right.

After slamming the door, Freddy scampered to the war room. He taped the letter to an altar, solemnly lit red and green Christmas candles that encircled it, banged a gong three times, and curled up on the floor waiting for sundown.

•••

Reverend LaFontaine and Faith finished their sundaes.

"Daddy, you have hot fudge on your chin."

He dabbed at it with his napkin. "All gone?"

She studied her father's soft brown eyes and inspected his chin. "All gone."

"Good, I want to look respectable. We still have two boxes of cookies to deliver: one to Mrs. Benson, and one to Mr. Nunn."

"Do you think I sold enough to win those tickets to Spooky World?"

"We won't know until Sunday after church. Let's go."

They drove home joyfully singing church hymns and telling Knock-Knock jokes. She scurried from the car to the kitchen and scooped up a box of cookies. "Mommy, did you give Dean his cookies?"

Grace lay dozing on the couch, covered with a soft blue blanket. "Aha," she murmured.

"Is it all right if I bring Mr. Nunn his cookies?"

"Where's Daddy?"

"He's out front talking with Mrs. Benson. She's crying because her cousin died. Can I go and deliver the cookies to Mr. Nunn?"

"Aha."

Faith tucked the cookies under her arm, tiptoed to her mother, and lightly touched her cheek. "I'll be right back, Mommy."

•••

At dusk Freddy awoke and struggled to his feet, groaning. He shook his leg and limped around the altar, pointing his finger at a statue of Guanyin. "You're no goddess of mercy. Why do you tell me to do this crap? It never works. Look, my hands are still shaking, and now my leg's numb. It's not supposed to be this way!" He whipped the tiny figure across the room. "Take that, you fat fraud!"

Nunn ran his tongue across his lips and rubbed his aching head. "Oh Judy, I can't do this by myself. I can't. If only you were here. If only you were here with me."

Freddy wiped his greasy hand across his mouth and anxiously approached the letter. It quivered in his trembling hands as he held it before the flickering candlelight. "I can't read this in here," he cried. "It's too dark!"

Frantically, he rushed downstairs to the living room, fumbled for the light switch, sank into a chair, and read his letter. A prickly chill spread throughout his body. Freddy Nunn gawked at the words, read them aloud, to himself, and, aloud again.

Sweat surged through every cell of his skin and clung to him like a killing frost. While his teeth chattered, his body shook and quaked until, suddenly, it stopped.

Nunn felt nothing. No words crossed his mind, and he moved no muscles. Quiet and alone he sat in the gathering dusk - his thoughts as bitter as a winter's wind - his soul as cold as ice.

A sound snapped his stupor. There it was again: a doorbell's chime seemed far and away, like some distant bell summoning to him. He sat alert and listening - *Yes it's calling my name all right and shooting through the telephone wires.*

He had heard the voice of Brigadier General John Thomas, who pulled up his charging horse, dismounted, and whispered in Freddy's ear, *"Answer the door, Soldier!"*

"Yes sir, I'll answer the door." He stood, saluted, and mechanically marched to the door.

Faith grinned and thrust the bright red box before his eyes. "Mr. Nunn, your cookies are here!" Freddy blinked at the box, but his gaze settled on Faith.

Her smile faded. "Are you all right, Mr. Nunn?" she asked cautiously stepping inside the hallway. "Mr. Nunn, are you sick?"

She looked into his vacant eyes and at the letter that hung from his hand.

"Mr. Nunn, is that the letter you've been waiting for?"

He offered her the letter, which she carefully slid from his hand, then sat on a musty sofa and read.

Her blue eyes sparkled. "It's a good thing I got an A in reading!"

Faith LaFontaine read the words tenderly and slowly. "Dear Mr. Nunn, We are pleased to inform you that your natural birth parents have been located in Massachusetts. Please see the attached documents for detailed information.

"In summary, your birth mother's name is Judith Cecelia Lydon. She is currently known as Judith Lydon Kennedy and resides in Braintree, Massachusetts. Your biological father, Glen Dwight Kelley, resides in South Boston"

"Shut up," hissed Freddy.

Faith shook her blonde head and laughed. "Are you just kidding with me, Mr. Nunn? Because our prayers have been answered. It says right here that your mother lives in Braintree."

"I know what it says, and I told you to shut up!" Freddy pressed his hands over his ears. "Shut up, just shut your mouth. Stop laughing and give me that letter!"

He stepped towards Faith and pressed his fist against her cheek. "Listen to me when I talk to you. I don't want to hear any more, so shut up!"

Freddy snatched the letter from her trembling hands.

Terrified by his bulging eyes and scarlet face, she froze.

His mouth glistened with saliva that spread over his chin and dripped onto his heaving chest. He shoved her head against the sofa and stumbled into a chair, his raging eyes pinned on her.

In that dingy room, Faith sat alone on the stinking sofa, struggling to hold back her tears. "Mr. Nunn, I wasn't laughing. I was smiling. I'm happy that your letter came. I'm sorry you didn't like it. But I need to go home now," she said, wringing her hands, "I told my mother that I'd be right back."

Nunn crossed his arms over his chest and glared at her. The general appeared again with a sword raised high above his head. *Tell her what you're going to do Freddy. Tell her!* Nunn's chest swelled with pride and he saluted his commanding officer. "Yes sir!"

Faith's face clouded in confusion. "Who are you talking to, Mr. Nunn?"

With a hazy stare, Freddy saw beyond her.

His voice softened, and he smiled at her. "You're evil, Faith, because your mother is evil - the cookies are poison. She had you sell them to me, and now you want me to eat them."

His face brightened as he leaned forward, slowly rubbing his hands together. "I'm a soldier, a *real* soldier fighting evil. I didn't know that about myself until I read the letter. Now everything is clear to me.

"You see Faith, I *thought* that I killed Judy and Ginger because they double crossed me, because they took all the money - because they were thieves and traitors trained by Alfred Locke.

"But that was before the letter. Now I know that I have special powers to see *real* wickedness ahead of time like, like, in the future. Like Judy trying to poison me with her evil ways. Like you trying to poison me with those cookies."

A bitter smile crossed his lips. "You know, Faith, evil touches evil, but now it can't touch me."

Tears dropped from her eyes and onto her reddened hands. "I'm not evil. I'm a good girl. There's no poison in the cookies, Mr. Nunn. Please, let me go home. I need to see my mother and father. They're waiting for me!"

"You're never going home. I need to finish my job," he said, sinking into a chair, tired, and heavy with sleep.

As he closed his eyes, Faith watched cautiously, stood, and raced to the door. He roused, bolted after her, grabbed her ponytail, and jerked her to the floor. "Take a break, Miss Priss. You're not going anywhere!"

Faith lay on the floor sobbing. "Mr. Nunn. I didn't mean to make you so mad. I'm sorry. I just read what was in the letter. I'm sorry about your mother. But I need to go home. I want my mother!"

Freddy circled her crumpled body. "*I want my mother, I want my mother*," he mimicked. "Didn't your father ever tell you about death? Because you're going to die!"

He wrestled her to the war room, shoved her in a closet, and locked the door.

CHAPTER FORTY

Reverend LaFontaine stood over his sleeping wife and anxiously shook her shoulder. "Grace, Grace, where's Faith?"

She turned a blank face to his and blinked at his question.

"Where's Faith, she's not home. I've looked everywhere!"

Grace yawned and sat up rubbing her eyes. "What do you mean you can't find her? She was going to deliver the cookies to Freddy's and come right home!"

"How long ago?"

"Oh, Lawrence, I'm sorry, I was napping." she said help-lessly. "I think Faith said that you were speaking with Mrs. Benson."

Lawrence nervously checked his watch. "She should be home by now. We need to start looking for her."

Grace stood but fell back on the sofa. "Oh, Lawrence," she cried, "my water broke. I'm soaked!"

"Any labor pains?"

"No, not yet," she sobbed.

"Lay back, Grace, lay back. I'll get you cleaned up. I'll call Mrs. Keith to come over. I've got to find Faith." Reverend Lawrence LaFontaine grabbed his flashlight and hurried to Freddy's in search of his daughter. A narrow beam streamed from his flashlight and shone through the dense shrubs and black shadows that surrounded the bleak house. Lawrence marched to the door and rang the bell. There was no answer. He rapped impatiently and waited. The porch light flicked on and the door flew open.

Freddy stood with his hands clasped over his belly. "Hello Reverend. What can I do you for?"

"Hello Mr. Nunn," he said breathlessly. "Has Faith been here? Did she deliver a box of cookies?"

"Yes, she did. And they are scrumptious, just delicious. I've eaten five of them already!"

Lawrence smiled weakly. "Well," he stammered, "she hasn't returned home yet and I was just wondering if she's still here?"

"My good heavens no, she left here some time ago. I'm not sure of the time, maybe half an hour or so. Have you checked with her little friends?"

Lawrence gulped and adjusted his glasses. "Well, no, not yet. I was hoping, well, that she was still here and just forgot about the time. May I use your phone?"

"Oh, hell's bells, wouldn't you know it. I can't find it!"

He studied Freddy's fidgeting hands and stepped forward. "May I come in?"

"No, no, you may not! I have a stomach virus. I've been on the toilet all day, and I think I need to go again!"

Lawrence flipped on the flashlight and quickly scanned the room.

"How dare you!" screamed Freddy knocking it from his hand.

He stooped to pick it up, and followed its yellow beam to the bright red box of cookies lying on the floor. "Are those the cookies you bought from my Faith? They don't look like they've been opened. You said you ate five. Where is she?"

Freddy's face darkened. "Reverend LaFon*fart*, your kid isn't the only one selling cookies!"

Lawrence nervously adjusted his glasses. "It's Reverend LaFon*taine*. I think my daughter's here, and I'm going to find her!"

"No, you're not!" Freddy snatched the glasses and whipped them across the room. He heaved the reverend against the door and rammed his head into his chest again and again, then shoved his knee into his groin. Lawrence groaned, buckled over and fell to the floor. Freddy seized the flashlight. "Here's something else for you!" he shouted and slammed it against his skull. "And here's a couple more for good luck!"

Reverend Lawrence Lafontaine moaned softly, gurgled, and lay still in a pool of bright, red blood.

CHAPTER FORTY ONE

Mrs. Keith carefully arranged tea and toast on a silver tray and regally carried it to the study.

"Mrs. Lafontaine, do keep your legs up. They're so swollen. I had the same problem with both my pregnancies. It was exhausting. Of course, that was in the '60s. Time may change things but not swollen feet and pregnancy. They go hand in hand.

"I remember going to the hairdresser's for a perm, and my stylist, Kippy, lifting my legs and placing them on a chair. He was just wonderful to me."

"I'm sure he was, Mrs. Keith. Please call me Grace."

"Well, all right, I'll call you Grace. Grace, you look warm, shall I open a window?"

"Yes, Mrs. Keith, please do."

Grace sat with a hand on her forehead, gratefully inhaling the crisp, night air.

"Now let's get a cool compress on your forehead."

"Thank you, Mrs. Keith. They're in the linen closet near the bathroom. I wonder what's keeping my husband. I need to get to the hospital!"

"I'm sure he'll be right along," she said, her soaring voice trailing down the hallway.

After returning, she laid the compress on Grace's forehead.

Wrinkling her nose, Mrs. Keith suddenly asked, "What is that odor?" as she followed its scent to an open window.

Grace shrugged. "You're asking the wrong person. I don't have a very good sense of smell."

Mrs. Keith furrowed her brows and inhaled deeply. "It's gasoline."

She sniffed again and pursed her lips. "Yes, its gasoline. Someone must be having trouble with their car."

"I haven't heard anything."

"Well, it's an awfully strong smell. I'll be right back. Keep an eye on me from the window."

Mrs. Keith zipped her jacket and left under the light of a full moon rising in the night sky.

Grace attempted to stand but quickly groped for the rocking chair. "Ah," she moaned gripping her abdomen. She stood hunched and shivering.

Mrs. Keith burst into the room. "Grace, which is Mr. Nunn's house? Is it next door, the one with all the trees and overgrown bushes around it?"

"Yes, that's it," she gasped. "Did you see Lawrence or Faith? What's wrong?"

"Oh, dear, I need to get you back on the couch," she said rushing towards Grace. "I don't want to alarm you, but there's something suspicious going on over there.

"I peeked through the bushes. A man is sprinkling something around his house and all over the yard from one of those gas cans, you know, the type you use to fill a lawn mower. I'm sure it's gasoline. We need to call the police!"

CHAPTER FORTY TWO

Nunn scrubbed gasoline from his hands and climbed the stairs to his war room. Pounding on the closet door, he hollered. "Faith, stop that crying or I'll really give you something to cry about. Now shut up!"

He adjusted his binoculars, scanned the neighborhood and causeway, re-adjusted the lens, and honed on Thomas Park. "Not too many of you little juvenile delinquents hanging around tonight screwing your girlfriends and pissing in the bushes.

"It's too cold for you, but not for Faith," he grumbled.

Freddy scrutinized the tall, white marble monument before shifting his focus to the huge maples on the hillside and the overgrown weeds and brush near the steepest slope where the tallest tree stood.

"Bingo, wingo," he mumbled. "Faith, you're going to be buried in Thomas Park - under the tallest tree."

He circled his replica of the monument and shifted the trees, placing the tallest to the bottom of the steepest slope. Nunn stroked a tiny soldier, Brigadier General John Thomas, and carefully re-positioned him high on the hill but behind a row of cannons and ahead of his soldiers, a spyglass pressed to his right eye searching for enemy movement.

Freddy prowled near the closet.

"Faith, stop crying. I'm going to take you for a ride to Thomas Park. It's in South Boston. Your father's downstairs. We're all going together, and then you're going home with him. I'm going to count to ten and open the door. If you're still crying, you can't come."

At ten, Nunn jerked open the door - Faith stood trembling in the darkness.

Nunn yanked out the terrified child, grabbed her chin, and peered down at her. "You've still got tears in your eyes. You can't come!"

Giggling, Freddy shoved her into the closet and locked its door.

"Have faith, Faith, that I'll be back. I'm going down to talk to your father."

Moving swiftly around Lafontaine's body, Nunn barricaded the doors and windows with furniture and panels of crumbling Sheetrock he hauled from the cellar.

"Don't bother getting up, LaFonfart," he said, scathingly. "I'm all set. Me and Faith are going for a ride. Keep an eye on the house for us. Oh, and, LaFonfart, don't forget the hot dogs and marshmallows. You're going to be hosting a barbeque tonight!"

Nunn trudged upstairs to his war room and fell against a wall, gasping for breath.

Sirens screaming from somewhere seized his attention, so he grabbed his binoculars and darted to the look-out.

Below, three cruisers with flashing blue lights swiftly sped through the night, heading across the causeway. He ran to an opposite window and watched as they screeched to a halt.

While cops hustled into LaFontaine's house, two more scanned Nunn's yard before running to the safety of their cruisers.

His telephone screamed. "Yes, Officer Boyden, this is Freddy Nunn. Why are you calling me? Yes, Faith and her father were here but they left a while ago. What's the problem? No, I don't know where they went, and I don't think gasoline is dangerous.

"This is private property, and I'm just killing weeds. If it's a safety hazard, tell my neighbors to move! What! You're not doing any such thing," he exclaimed. "The fire department isn't getting near my yard. You tell them to stay away from here!" he hollered and slammed down the phone.

As he loaded his rifle to the frantic blur of flashing red lights and ear-splitting sound of sirens, Nunn's breaths came rapidly.

CHAPTER FORTY
THREE

A full moon, fat and yellow sailed higher and higher through the navy blue of the night sky - hundreds of thousands of miles above Deputy Hugh Drinkwater and his yellow-coated crew of firefighters who scrambled around their bright red trucks.

"Gear up and get your air masks on," he barked.

"Get out of here!"

Drinkwater stopped short.

"I'm up here, Bozo!"

He stepped back and followed the voice to an attic window.

"Call your water weasels off and get the hell out of here!"

Deputy Drinkwater cupped his hands around his mouth and hollered, "Mr. Nunn, we've received a complaint. Would you please come to the door? You're in violation of code! The State of Massachusetts strictly prohibits the use of gasoline for…"

Nunn struck a match to a candlewick that sputtered and spat before bursting into flame.

"Hey, Deputy Super Squirt, take a look at this!"

Drinkwater's jaw dropped and he spun around and dashed for the truck. "Charge the lines! Charge the lines! Get that water moving!"

Freddy slid the rifle's barrel over the window and fired.

Drinkwater dropped to the ground.

Grace jumped. "Oh, no. Was that a gunshot?"

The police bolted out the door and slunk behind their cruiser.

Officer Boyden switched on. "Fireman shot, fireman down, gasoline on ground and yard, father and daughter missing - could be in house with shooter!"

"We'll mobilize tactical," the dispatcher replied.

Nunn raced to the war room and threw open the closet door. Faith darted past him, but Freddy tackled her to the floor.

She struggled beneath his weight, his hot breath gusted in her face. "You try that again, and I'll kill you now!" He bound her hands behind her back, sealed her mouth with duct tape, and dragged her across the room.

"You see that door? There's a porch out there; it's called a widow's walk. You can watch the sailboats from there, and that's where you're going - but not to watch the sailboats, but to sail like they do, but not in the water. You're going to sail right over the railing!"

Her blue eyes growing wide with terror, Faith shuddered and shook her head, *No, no, no!*

"Tough luck, Miss Priss. Your father's dead. And your mother can't help you. No one can!" He bound her ankles and grabbed a rope, but hastily threw it down.

"What's that noise?"

The amplified voice of a negotiator cut through the crisp night air and sea of flickering red and blue lights below him. Nunn ducked from the blinding light that swept back and forth across his house.

Again the voice boomed. "Freddy, I'm Joe, Joe Flynn. I'm here to help. Can you meet me at the front door? Can we talk?"

"For starters, you can turn that fog horn down. It's giving me a headache!"

"Will do, Freddy, wasn't sure if you could hear me. Is that better? Can you still hear me?"

"Of course, I can. The whole neighborhood can hear it!"

"Freddy, there's gasoline down here. Can you snuff that candle and throw down that rifle so we can talk?"

Nunn disappeared but returned in a flash. "It's out!"

"Where's the gun?"

"It's not a gun, Columbo, or should I say, Dumbo. It's a rifle, and I'm not giving it up. I need to protect myself!"

"Who or what do you need to protect yourself from - Faith and her father? Why are you holding them in there?"

"How do you know that?"

"A neighbor saw them go in and said they never came out."

"Faith's going over the widow's walk," he shrieked. "And her daddyo is as dead as a doornail. I've got my orders."

While a SWAT team scouted the yard, Joe's voice echoed in the night. "Let's back up for a minute. Want to tell me about it?"

Pulling and twisting his sweat-soaked hair, Freddy paced in frenzied circles. He called for General John Thomas, but he had disappeared.

"I can't tell you about it, but it was all so evil, Joe. It was all so evil. I was tricked. I prayed and prayed, but it came out all wrong!"

"Freddy, you *can* tell me about it. That's what I'm here for. I can help. What happened, who tricked you? Who gave you orders?"

"If I tell you, Joe, you'll take me to jail!"

"I can't take you anywhere. I'm here to help you. Take a chance with me."

Freddy crumpled the letter from the adoption agency and threw it out the window. "Read that."

Joe got the "nod," hustled over and recovered the gasoline soaked letter. "Freddy, I can't read it. Tell me about it. Tell me. I'm listening!"

"I killed my mother!" he moaned. "I didn't know she was my mother until the letter came. And I slept with her. I slept with my own mother! She was a wicked woman - evil like Ginger! Like Alfred Locke.

"They stole my share of money. They laughed at me, used me! I thought that I was protected from evil, but I wasn't. So I killed both of them! I took care of it myself!"

Static voices crackled and hissed from fire trucks and squad cars - far below the rhythmic chop of a swooping helicopter. Fortified behind trees, trucks, and squad cars lawmen kept their eyes and ears on Joe.

"Freddy, if you were tricked, then you're a victim, too, a victim of circumstance. A great wrong has been done to you. But we can work it out. You have the power, Freddy. You have the power to stop Faith from becoming a victim. You can stop the cycle of evil, Freddy - say yes to it. Let Faith go home. And then we'll talk about Judy and Ginger."

"Don't try to trick me!" he screamed. "Faith is evil too. She tried to poison me with cookies, and she laughed at me. Everyone laughs at me!"

"Freddy, she's only a little girl. She's afraid, that's all. Sometimes what we see isn't the real deal. We can work this out. Come on, Freddy, let's talk about it. Trust me, Freddy, trust me!"

"Joe, you're just talk, talk, talk - trying to talk me right into jail, jail, jail. And I'm no traitor. Forget about it!" he shouted.

Nunn aimed and fired at the street lights, dropped his rifle, scrambled to the war room, and hauled Faith to the widow's walk.

The pines and oaks loomed tall and dark and safely shrouded the swarm of sharpshooters hiding in the shadows.

Tactile called the team commander. "We can't cover that widow's walk. It recedes under the overhang and faces east. The yard is wide open, and there's no cover out there. Its high tide, and we've got six-mile-per-hour winds - perfect weather to take the shooter out seaside."

"All right, I'll call Gillan and have you and one of the sharp-shooters hook-up at the launch. You can travel by police boat to the east side of the house. You'll have plenty of cover from the ledge. Gillan knows the terrain. I'll have Joe keep talking. You guys have forty-five minutes to get in position."

Joe lifted the bullhorn. "Freddy, come to the window. Talk to me. I can help you. Problems have solutions."

Freddy cupped his hands around his mouth and screamed, "The only solution is for you to pack up your horn and go home!"

"We're not going anywhere. You've got two innocent people in there. We've got you surrounded."

"I'll light this place on fire - it'll go up like a bomb!"

"We've got firemen here. They're ready. Do the right thing. Come on out. I'm here for you."

Slowly, Freddy slid against the wall, groaning and weeping. "Why was I ever born? Oh why was I ever born?"

•••

Grace lay on her bed, panting and moaning.

"Push!" ordered the officer. "Push! You're doing good. I can see it! I can see it! I can see the top of his head!"

"I can't. I can't," she gasped. "I'm so tired."

"I said push, push. You're almost there!"

She sucked in her breath and exhaled in agony.

Wringing her hands, Mrs. Keith asked, "Officer Steves, are you sure we can't leave the house and get her to the hospital?"

"I told you, a shooter is unpredictable. If they're spooked they'll fire. We've got to sit tight!"

From the look on Grace's face, Steves knew she was terrified. "We're going to get your family out of there. Don't worry, just breathe and push!"

Mrs. Keith hovered around Grace. "I'll bring more warm water and towels."

"And bring scissors and some string. Michael Vincent is on his way!"

CHAPTER FORTY FOUR

Sharpshooter J. D., adjusted his gear, heartily slapped Gillan's back, and hustled onto an awaiting police boat, quickly followed by his spotter, Marty.

"Good to see you again, Gillan," he said in a husky, Southern drawl. "Let's move."

The able craft sped across the bay under the glow of the full moon, its reflection dancing on the rippling water churning by the boat's wake.

Gillan winced at an annoying ring from his cell. "This is Gillan. Marybeth, I can't talk. We've got a hostage situation going on. I'll call you later. And don't wait up."

He pushed forward the throttle, and the boat accelerated. As the sharpshooters geared up, the phone rang again. "This is Gillan. Hey, Christine, what's up?"

Gillan listened briefly. "Christine, I can't talk long, but I think you've been on the right track. I'm on the boat heading to Freddy Nunn's - a hostage situation. I'll talk with you later."

•••

Christine threw on a jacket and sped to Freddy's, but the police had blocked the causeway. "Do you live up here?" a trooper asked.

"No," she sighed and turned her car around. She pulled alongside a marsh and watched a helicopter fly into search lights sweeping through the night sky. She did not see Gillan's boat skimming across the bay.

He reduced speed to a dead idle and nearly floated over the marsh grass.

After grabbing their gear and wading to the stony shore, the sniper and his spotter climbed over a rock-strewn slope towards a ledge. Marty lay low but edged higher. He pulled out his binoculars, studied the widow's walk and the terrain around it, measured the wind's velocity, and calculated his angle and range.

J. D. brashly assembled his rifle and adjusted the settings to Marty's calculations.

"Hmm, an M40?"

"It's the only way to go, man," he said while stroking its barrel.

He set the weapon on a bipod, peered through the lens, and saw the widow's walk in its crosshairs.

J.D. rolled on his side, feeling the ground.

Marty whispered. "What's wrong?"

"I've got a damn rock sticking into my stomach."

CHAPTER FORTY FIVE

F reddy Nunn ran from the staccato calling of his name and thundered into his war room. His blood boiled at the sight of the silent little soldiers.

Seizing an ancient sword from its sheath he smashed it on the table. "You spies," he shrieked. "You traitors have got me surrounded! You'll get yours!"

Nunn's fury stormed on with every belt and bang of the blade, as he slashed and swooped the sword across the soldiers and sent them scattering.

He scooped the small marble monument and whipped it across the room. "Take that, General John Thomas!"

"Break! Break! Why won't you break, why won't you break?" he cried, again hurling the monument against the wall. Sinking to the floor and groveling in the dark, Nunn found the piece, raced to the widow's walk, pitched it over the rail, and dashed inside.

Gripping the sword, Freddy faced the altar. "And, you, you are a lie, the most evil of all lies!" he screamed, whipping and slicing into the paper silhouette of his know known mother.

Freddy grabbed a gun, jammed it under his belt, and fumed while pounding on the closet door. "You're next Faith!"

He tore her from the closet and shoved her against the wall. "You stand up! Stand up, I said!"

Faith's eyes rolled back, and she crumbled to the floor. He ran to the widow's walk and wailed into the night, "She's going over. She's going over the railing!"

Marty adjusted his focus.

Joe's amplified voice pierced the night air: "Freddy, Freddy, stop! Let's talk!"

"Shut up! I can't stand the sound of your voice! Here's all the talking I'm going to do!"

Exploding bullets whizzed by Joe's head. "Faith's going to where she belongs - to hell!"

Hauling Faith to the railing, he shrieked, "Stand up! Stand up! Or I'll shoot you right here."

Freddy clung to the railing, gasping and frantically waving his gun over Faith. "You're going to die, you're going to die!"

The commander gave the order, and Marty nodded to J. D. "Now."

"His head's bobbing. I'm going for mid-sternum. Imminent death to you - you crazy bastard!" J.D. exhaled, held still, and fired.

"It's a hit!"

Stunned, Freddy fell forward, collapsed on the railing, and hung there like a rag.

The steady chop of the helicopter echoed through the dark night, and its guiding light lingered on Freddy Nunn's lifeless body.

When the railing yielded to his weight, Freddy's body slithered slowly off the highest roof dropped into a crumpled ball on the second, slipped some more, fell onto the steep gable of the first, picked up speed, and finally slammed into the ground!

J.D. kissed the muzzle of his M40; Marty gave him a sociable slap on the back.

EPILOGUE

Doctor Ed Khan's surgical mask hung from his face and dipped beneath his chin. "Mrs. LaFontaine, your husband suffered a subdural hematoma. The surgery went fine. He'll be in intensive care for a few days, and then we'll move him to a bed on the neuro-surgical floor."

"The neuro-surgical floor? I'm sorry, doctor; I'm not quite sure what that means."

"Oh, sorry about that," he grinned. "It means that the nurses working there specialize in caring for patients who've had surgery to their brain. Your husband had a blood clot, but not anymore."

"Oh, of course. Thank you doctor."

Dr. Khan bolted from the room but returned a moment later. "Oh, Mrs. LaFontaine, my mother just paged me and asked that I tell you that she'll be up in a few minutes to discuss your daughter's injuries. Nothing to be alarmed about, a few scratches and a sprained finger.

"They have a social worker and a policeman in talking with her right now. Your daughter is a trooper! She's doing great. My mother said that the emergency room is pretty busy right now, full moon, I guess."

"Thank you, Doctor Khan. So you and your mother work in the same hospital? Your mother works in the emergency department?"

"It's a family affair. My mother, Saima Khan, is a trauma specialist here in the hospital, and my father is head of orthopedics. My brother, David, is an urologist, but he's out in Utah."

Mrs. Keith laughed. "Oh, then you and David work on opposite ends of the body. Well, we're glad you're here tonight, Dr. Khan. We needed a good brain man, not a bladder man!"

Grace nodded. "Yes, that's for sure. Thank you, Dr. Khan."

He waved briskly and dashed down the hall.

Mrs. Keith shook her head. "They're always in such a hurry."

"Yes, they are," Grace agreed, wiping the tears from her eyes and gently stroking her tiny son's cheek. "I don't know what I would've done without you, Mrs. Keith. You, Dr. Khan, and Officer Steves have all been wonderful to me. I'm so grateful."

"Now, now, I'm sure you'd do as much for us. It's been a night to remember. I'm retired, you know, and it sure did pick up the pace of my life. I was supposed to be stocking shelves at the food pantry!"

Grace cuddled Michael closer. "I guess we all thought we'd be doing something else. Mrs. Keith, have you heard how the fireman is who was shot?"

She chuckled. "Oh, him. I ran into his wife in the emergency room. She sings in the choir. He refuses to worship. Anyway, not to worry. He was shot in the butt and played possum until they dragged him to safety. I bet he'll be in church in a few weeks singing his praises and thanking the Almighty!"

Mrs. LaFontaine leaned into the pillow and let out a breath. "I'm so relieved and so happy for his family.

"Well, Grace, I'm just getting started. Do you know Linda Locke? She's new to the church."

"Yes, I've seen the name, but I haven't been so involved the past couple of months," she said, looking at the baby.

"Well, her husband, Alfred Locke, is President of the Quincy Quarry Bank and Trust. They made a donation to the church and helped us buy the new piano from Carretta's Music Store. Elio, the owner, is quite a musician you know.

"Anyway, Linda told me that Alfred had some type of a shock to his body and was on life support. He's talking now and breathing on his own. He's such a good and decent man, a real pillar of the community, the type of person you can really trust. We need to put him on our prayer list."

•••

Gillan gave a hearty handshake to Marty and slapped J. D. on the back. The men grabbed their gear and left to join their team. Gillan removed Ronan's protective gear and life preserver and packed them with his own.

He scribbled a few notes in his log, called Chung to confirm a meeting for the next day, started his car, and punched in Christine's number. "It's all over. Freddy Nunn admitted to killing Judy and Ginger. Guess they were all in on the bank theft. The little girl and her father are okay.

"I just spoke with Chung. Locke's going to make it, so Sweede and Ted will question him when he's ready, it seems he was in on it too. Freddy must have framed Will Kennedy. Anyway, our sniper took him out. You'll get the whole story after we talk with Locke.

"Got to go. Talk with you later."

Marybeth sorted through wedding pictures of herself and Gillan. Moving the album from her lap to the table, she hurried to answer the phone.

"Gillan, are you all right? How did everything go? I've been worried sick. It did? You must be exhausted! I made a meatloaf. I thought I'd make sandwiches for our trip to Maine, if everything went well. You must be hungry.

"I'll have a nice warm sandwich and a cold glass of beer waiting for you. And I chilled your favorite glass."

•••

Christine glanced at her wristwatch and called Charlie Sudanski.

"God Almighty! You couldn't make that stuff up. And you guessed that Freddy and Judy were related because they both had a space in their front teeth. Unbelievable!" he said.

He paused, then added, "No, I don't think Judy Kennedy knew that Freddy was her son. The DA will contact the agency that gave the adoption information to Freddy. There must be some evidence on his computer. They'll have records of inquiry. They'll know if Judy tried to find Freddy, but I doubt it.

"She was crazy, but I don't think she was twisted enough to sleep with her own son. Christine, I have to get to the airport, I'll be home tomorrow afternoon.

"Have fun breaking the news to Will in the morning."

•••

Kennedy laid in his cell reading and waiting for the breakfast bell when a cranky voice of a guard called to him. "Hey, Kennedy, your lawyer's downstairs in the conference room. Pack up. You're getting out."

As the sun streamed through open windows, Christine signed papers in the morning light when Will stepped inside the room. Their eyes locked for a moment.

The DA's team spoke with Will and slid his paperwork across the table for him to sign. Once done, he slid it back.

"Can I give you a ride home, Will?"

"Are you driving?"

"Hop in."

In awkward silence, they rode across town but merely inched through Boston's heavy morning traffic, and ignored exhaust fumes, horns blowing, and screaming sirens.

Will looked at the skyline and a plane flying from Logan and wondered where it was headed. Fumbling with the paperwork on his lap, he turned to Christine, "It's a beautiful day."

"Yes, yes, it is. I'm glad that I took it off."

He hesitated. "Do you have any plans?"

Christine glanced into his eyes. "No, Will, no, I don't."

"Would you like to grab a coffee? We could drive over to Carson Beach, maybe go for a walk?"

"All right. That sounds good."

They passed G Street and the monument on Thomas Park, which rose bright and white against the clearest of blue skies, and found a parking space near the statue of Father Joseph LaPorte.

After coffee, they stepped into the late September sunshine and the cool, clean, scent of salt air that blew in from Dorchester Bay.

Will and Christine strolled in silence along the deserted beach. The outgoing tide had washed away broken shells, pebbles, and shreds of seaweed that had washed ashore with the night's tide.

Will glanced at Christine and then looked ahead. The beach lay wide open and glistening in the morning sun, and the sand, soft and smooth beneath their feet, seemed to stretch ahead and to forever.

"Christine, you're awfully quiet. Would you like to keep walking?"

She followed his gaze from the shimmering sands ahead to the horizon and reached for his hand. "Yes, Will, let's keep walking."

ACKNOWLEDGEMENTS

B ob Gillan allowed me to take advantage of his life's work and knowledge of bad guys, munitions, and detection dogs. Bob patiently answered my questions until I finally understood and then hooked me up with Jim Lundgren. He put an unloaded weapon in my hands and provided insight into the work of a police sniper.

Robert Pearson took my endless telephone calls regarding all things naval.

Mike Hussey helped me navigate through Stellwagen Bank via the Internet.

The librarians at the Thomas Crane Public Library in Quincy, Massachusetts, were indispensable.

Gary Banuk, Joe Verlicco and Paul O'Connell provided me with the answers to issues I could not figure out on my own.

Lee and Chucky Kennedy were inspiring and walked with me through the streets of South Boston and around Thomas Park to help me gain a fuller understanding of the culture there during the '60's.

George Verlicco, an avid sports fan, liked the idea of Bullet Hayes.

Kris Bopp, Al Darois, Judy Keith, Suzanne and Jamie Tapper, Tom Pittsley, Michael Pugliesi and Tony Volpe cheered me on.

Editor Richard Connolly's commitment and skill made all the difference.

Mary Gaynor, a wonderful friend with a passion for music and literature graciously made the time to proof read this book.

Paula Bonomi-DiCesare, a resourceful and intelligent friend, brain stormed with me for the title to this book.

Elio Carretta listened to me.

For more information regarding Stellwagen Bank, contact: stellwagen.noaa.gov

I am grateful to all for taking the time to help me realize this story.

31558858R00159

Made in the USA
Charleston, SC
22 July 2014